PRAISE FOR

the tiger saga

"Warning: these books may cause you to forget anything else exists
until you've turned the last enthralling page. And then you'll want
to start all over again!"
—BREE DESPAIN, author of *The Dark Divine* trilogy

"The way Colleen weaves Indian culture, Hinduism, and her own
made-up fairy tale into an action-packed love story is captivating."
—MTV.com's HOLLYWOOD CRUSH blog

"Houck's first novel is part Indiana Jones and part fairy tale . . .
she tells a good story that will keep readers turning pages."
—BOOKLIST

the tiger saga

tiger's promise

tiger's promise

by COLLEEN HOUCK

For my brothers—Mel, Andrew, and Jared—

Challenging opponents in board games

but devoted supporters in life

contents

early death

Hartley Coleridge 1796–1849

SHE pass'd away like morning dew
Before the sun was high;
So brief her time, she scarcely knew
The meaning of a sigh.

As round the rose its soft perfume,
Sweet love around her floated;
Admired she grew—while mortal doom
Crept on, unfear'd, unnoted.

Love was her guardian Angel here,
But Love to Death resign'd her;
Tho' Love was kind, why should we fear
But holy Death is kinder?

prologue: thwarted

Most little girls looked forward to the time when their father returned home. Yesubai did not. As soon as the clanging bell announced his arrival, fear seized her heart in a powerful grip and the young girl stopped breathing.

No one who took note of the small child could tell how deathly terrified she actually was. All one could see was a diminutive princess, adorned in the finest of silks. Her large, unusual-colored lavender eyes, framed by thick, dark eyelashes, set in a heart-shaped face, made even the crossest of hearts melt. On the outside, she was as calm and as still as a mountain lake. There was nothing of the shrewd and the mysterious about her, at least not outwardly. Yesubai's demeanor reflected nothing of her father.

Despite this, not one soul who worked closely with the family would risk so much as a whisper regarding the possibility of indiscretions on the part of their master's late wife. No one was that stupid. They thought it though. They all wondered how such a rare gem could come forth from a fount so impure. None pondered this idea more than Yesubai's beloved caretaker, Isha.

The servant woman, Isha, had been called in almost immediately upon the death of the master's wife, Yuvakshi. Isha had, in fact, been friends with the midwife who helped deliver Yuvakshi's baby, but soon after the birth of her young ward, the unfortunate death of Yuvakshi was announced. This was quickly followed by the midwife's mysterious disappearance. Isha, a nursemaid, was hired, and she and the young baby girl were banished to the far side of the sumptuous home in the small kingdom of Bhreenam.

Bhreenam had once been a peaceful place to live. Their king was old but he was a good man with very few political ambitions. Most of the people were herders and farmers, and the military was just large enough to provide security from the occasional rabble-rouser or drunkard. It was a good place to live. Once.

Now a new military commander had taken over. The very man who had hired Isha. He was a dark man. A dangerous one. Outwardly, of course, he was all smiles, and to the king he played at deference, but it was all Isha could do not to chant a plea to the gods to ward off evil every time he came near. Her employer frightened her. More than anyone she'd ever met.

Isha's suspicion that the young baby's father had done something terrible to his wife was amplified when he visited the nursery. She'd often enter the room to find him staring down at the young baby with naked loathing on his face. Like a coward, she'd wait in the doorway, half hidden and wringing her hands as she whispered silent supplications that the little girl who she'd come to love would not do anything to upset her father.

When he'd leave, she'd breathe a sigh of relief and thank the gods for keeping her ward asleep through the ordeal. But after each of his visits, she'd discover the little girl was awake after all, her liquid eyes still staring at the spot where her father's face had recently been. The baby's little limbs were still, and her blanket remained tightly tucked around her.

Later, despite the frequent appearance of the baby's father, Isha would want the girl to show more emotion; in fact, she often wondered if something was wrong with her charge. She wasn't a mean child. It was nothing of that sort. Yesubai just had a serious nature.

She didn't play as other children did. Instead of daydreaming or playacting with her toys, she merely propped them up in a place that she said displayed them in the best light. Her smiles were rare. Though her beauty was undeniable, most saw her as merely a pretty doll. Only Isha could sense the deep feelings that ran beneath the surface.

The visits from Yesubai's father became less frequent as the child grew older, and most of the time, he left his daughter alone, the exception being when he trotted her out for political assemblies and parties. The child's rare beauty seemed to please him then, especially when it was remarked upon by the king. Yesubai followed her father from minister to minister, even holding his hand when he demanded it, and made not a sound unless she was directly addressed. Even then, she was as polite and as perfect as a princess, and her quiet nature charmed all who met her.

Though he used her to his advantage, Yesubai's father spoke not a kind word to her and passed the girl off as soon as was immediately possible. Only when ensconced safely in Isha's arms did the young girl's shoulders droop and her beautiful eyes flutter closed. Isha would then tuck the little ethereal creature into bed and wonder, not for the first time, if she was a grown woman, wise beyond her years, trapped in the body of a little girl.

When Yesubai was eight, her father departed for a trip he'd been strangely excited about. The gleam in his eyes was frightening, and Isha secretly hoped that whatever compelled him to leave would somehow keep him away indefinitely, but, as always, he returned, and she waited with crippling fear for the aftermath. If her master's trip had gone well, he'd have the servants deliver boxes of cut flowers, but if it had gone badly, he'd seek out Yesubai personally. Isha didn't have to wait long.

When she bustled into the room, she saw the little girl she'd come to love standing immobile and staring at the door. She took the hand of her charge and squeezed lightly. Lavender eyes blinked once, twice, and then she looked up at the old servant woman. The tiniest lift at the corner of her mouth indicated to Isha that Yesubai was grateful for her presence.

As Yesubai carefully covered her waist-length hair with a purple scarf, Isha bustled around the already pristine room and slid a book an inch lower on the table, wiped condensation from the cold flask of water, straightened a blanket, and fluffed a few pillows.

The stomp of heavy boots was heard in the hallway, and quickly Yesubai secured her scarf across her face so that only her lovely eyes could be seen. Isha took her place off to the side of the room and hovered in the shadows, steeling herself to protect her ward but secretly hoping it wouldn't be necessary. As much as Isha wanted to be a strong woman, one who would not bow down to evil, she always felt the guilty relief that came when the little girl who knew too much was able to handle her father on her own.

Someday, she thought. Someday, I will stand fearless beside her.

But Isha did not stand fearless beside Yesubai, at least not right away. As the girl's father entered the room, power crackling at his fingertips, both the girl and the old woman knew that the visit that day would not bring flowers but thorns. As Yesubai curtsied for her father and diminutively lowered her eyes in the way he expected, he lashed out—first with the unnatural power stored up in his arms, and then with his fists.

Precious silks went up in flames. Chunks of stone blew away

from the wall and crashed into the opposite one. Little dolls with intricately carved wax faces melted into puddles. When the physical destruction proved ineffective in calming his temper, he finally turned on his daughter.

Bravely, she stood before him, head bowed and calm while he raged about the things he wanted but were just out of his grasp—such as his lust for a woman who spurned him, the fact that Yesubai was a cowering weakling, and that her birth had denied him the son he so very much wanted at his side.

With the rage of a bull, he drew back his arm and struck Yesubai across the face with so much strength that the force picked up her thin frame. The wind tossed her veil aside and whipped her hair. With a sickening smack, Yesubai hit the wall and slid slowly down, crumpling into a heap on the floor. The little girl lay still, her broken body hung like a lifeless doll tossed carelessly over jagged pieces of stone.

With a cry, Isha rushed forward into the path of the monster only to be rewarded with a broken leg, a crushed windpipe, two blackened eyes, and deep purple bruises down her body. Her ward was dead and Isha knew she would be soon joining her.

In the quiet after his departure, she wakened. Pain licked her limbs and pounded beneath her eyelids, and yet she sensed a fluttering touch on her arm. Yesubai. The girl was alive.

She touched her beloved caretaker with tender, tentative fingers, and a warm tingle soothed the pain that arced through Isha's limbs. Hours passed and, as she healed, Isha pondered the things she'd been able to glean from her master's rants. It seemed he had recently failed in an attempt to infiltrate a neighboring kingdom, which spurred his rage. He'd screamed that the amulets would belong to him and that if he had to go through a thousand soldiers to get his hands on the young princes, then so be it.

As he'd beaten his daughter, he'd said that she was worthless and as docile as her mother and that a powerful man such as himself needed a strong and compelling woman to stand at his side. He said he'd only wished he'd killed Yuvakshi before she'd given him a mewling daughter to be the thorn in his side.

Isha lay quietly, the swelling in her face and body subsiding thanks to Yesubai's healing touch, but the young girl, with bleeding cuts from her father's rings marring her beautiful face, cried and softly apologized, saying that there wasn't much she could do to help with the leg. It didn't matter. Isha would heal enough.

The limp she had following that day was a reminder for Isha to stand firm against evil. It actually gave her a sense of pride to know that she'd been brave enough to defend her ward after all. Yet, as heroic as she'd been that day, she still desperately feared the future. What would her master do when he learned that the two of them had not died?

On that day full of pain and sorrow, Isha came to understand two very important things.

First—there was a magic, darkly used by the father, which had been somehow passed on to the daughter. And second—Yesubai's father had indeed killed his late wife and would not hesitate to murder again. She'd suspected him of the blackest evil before, but now she knew that he was capable of worse. Much worse.

1

Veil

I sat at the mirror as Isha brushed out my hair in smooth strokes and fingered the petals of the yellow flowers I'd just arranged. My father had returned from a successful campaign, one that opened new avenues for acquiring wealth. Not that the people or the king would ever see a golden coin, a fat sheep, or even a bolt of precious fabric. No. The only ones who would profit from my father's exploits would be his close supporters—men nearly as vile, deceitful, and corrupt as he was.

Of course no one actually came close to perpetrating the deeds he had. If I were, in fact, to compare the leches' doings side by side against the acts of villainy performed by my father, they would all fall short. I'd long ago stopped counting the number of people he'd had killed in the most violent of ways. If it hadn't been for Isha, I would have quietly disappeared years ago.

Unfortunately, the magic I'd been able to hone only applied to myself, other than the little bit of healing I'd been able to provide for Isha over the years—a skill we carefully kept secret. We both knew the danger we'd be in if my father ever found out I was in possession of even a drop of the magic he possessed. So the two of us watched and waited, but there was never a time when we weren't surrounded, never a time when a guard wasn't at his most attentive. They all knew what would happen to them should they fail my father. Until such time as our circumstances changed, we were trapped.

I was always careful, always vigilant, but even more so now that he'd returned. It was my sixteenth birthday, and the king, as kind a man as my father was contemptible, had requested my presence at a celebration. He was throwing an elaborate party and, though I was grateful for his thoughtfulness in inviting me, my stomach twisted with nerves.

When the festivities were announced, I inwardly cringed, knowing the activity would require me to be on the arm of my father, a position I loathed, but even worse, it was a position that was inherently dangerous. Still, to mark the day of my birth by attending a lavish event at the palace was a special and rare enough affair that I looked forward to the occasion regardless. Especially because I thought I just might get an opportunity to visit the king's famous garden.

Isha announced that my hair was finished. She'd artfully arranged it so the bulk of it hung down my back, but she'd pinned up several sections at my crown and affixed little jewels among the strands. Attired in sumptuous yet as markedly modest silks as my father would allow, I presented myself for Isha's inspection.

She clucked her tongue. "You were always a beautiful child, my little Yesubai, but you are becoming a breathtaking young woman."

Taking the sheer veil from her hands, I wrapped it around my back, placed it carefully over my hair, and gave her a hint of a sad smile. "And you know how much I wish I was of a plainer appearance. Beauty only serves to draw more of his attention."

As she pinned the veil in place, Isha countered, "Perhaps your beauty stays his hand more often than is in his nature."

"Perhaps." I fixed the lower portion of the sheer golden veil across my face, felt the telltale twinge in my stomach that meant someone of great power was nearby, and said, "He approaches. Secret yourself in the closet."

"Yes, mistress." Isha cupped my cheek with her soft, wrinkled hand. "Be safe tonight."

I patted her arm. "You as well."

Isha turned quickly, taking the brush with her, and limped away. For a large woman with a bad leg, she moved silently, a proficiency we had both mastered out of necessity. Though I listened carefully, even I could not hear an indication that she was present. From the closet, she would be able to see the exchange between me and my father, but she had implicit instructions not to intervene no matter what happened.

The likelihood that he would heap abuse upon me before we met the king was minimal anyway, and even if he did, I could heal myself, whereas my ability to heal any injury she sustained was limited. If only I could practice my magic more openly, perhaps I could attain a level of power strong enough to be of real help.

Steeling myself, I lowered my eyes at the precise moment the door opened. My father entered the room with his aide, Hajari, a man as vicious as he was ugly. Standing rooted in place, I subdued the flinch as Hajari closed the door behind him and felt the hum of energy in my body as I purposely relaxed my limbs.

"And where is your lazy nursemaid?" my father, Lokesh, immediately questioned. "She has a bad habit of leaving you alone too long."

"I am never truly alone, Father," I said softly and felt the frown of his annoyance. I'd been careless in my comment. It smacked of boldness. Quickly, I added, "Besides, there is not a soul living in the house of my esteemed father who would dare to approach me with malevolent intention. Your powerful influence is felt even from a distance."

After a moment of intent scrutiny, he decided to let my comment pass. "That is as it should be," he said impatiently.

"It was perhaps rash of me," I voiced quickly, "but I sent Isha to bed early. She is feeling sickly, and I did not wish to attend the king with a sniveling, unsightly red nose."

He grunted but immediately lost interest in Isha. My father deplored weakness above all things and detested seeing it in others. As long as I'd known him, he'd never taken ill, but any soldier who so much as coughed in his vicinity was immediately sent away from his presence. His aversion to sickness worked in my favor, but I knew he was far too intelligent for me to use that particular trick again.

Circling me, he boldly appraised my appearance, and though my hands clenched when I saw Hajari's vile leer displaying his blackened and broken teeth—something he only dared to do behind my father's turned back—I quickly opened my fingers and smoothed my skirts. It would not do to show my father I felt fear or nerves. He loved nothing more than invoking the emotion in others. Even Hajari's face was impassive when my father circled around.

"I suppose you are attired appropriately," my father said. "Though you know I prefer lavender to this gold. It brings out your eyes." He cupped my chin and I obediently lifted my gaze to meet his.

"I will remember your preferences for the next celebration we attend," I murmured demurely but with just enough cheek that his instinct to exploit weakness would not be triggered. We both knew that another royal invitation was unlikely at best.

My father was like a beast of prey. If a person was bold enough to stand up to him, he admired the gesture, but if he considered a person too weak, he simply destroyed him. The best way to avoid being caught between his jaws was to leave no tracks, to move through the space like a spirit.

I was ten when I discovered I had the ability to vanish. At first, I didn't even know what had happened. The stomping of boots outside my door frightened me, and I froze in place. Isha came quickly into my chamber, rushing past, straightening up my already immaculate room. My father preferred his possessions, as he did his people—though to him people were possessions—to all be in their proper places should he wish to find them.

Isha's precautions had been unnecessary. The door never opened. When she peeked outside, she conversed briefly with the guard and then closed the door.

That's when she started calling my name. "Bai? Yesubai? Where are you? You can come out now. Your father is away. It was just the changing of the guard."

"I…I'm right here," I whispered softly.

"Bai? Where are you? I cannot see you."

"Isha?" Concerned, I stepped forward, placing my hand on her arm. She let out a panicked squeak and ran her hands over my arms and face.

"It must be the magic," she said. "You've made yourself invisible. Can you change back?"

"I don't know," I answered, the panic blooming in my chest.

"Try clearing your mind. Think of something meaningless."

"Like what?"

Isha looked at the boxes of flowers that had just been brought in from the market for me to arrange—the one pleasure my father allowed me. As I cupped each lovely bud, I imagined it growing wild in the sun as it stretched its leaves toward the sky, even though

I knew that most of the flowers brought to me were cultivated. Watching the blooms slowly wither over time felt oddly appropriate and extremely prophetic.

I wondered, even as a child, when my own bloom would fade and I, too, would waste away into nothing in my chamber, where I could draw no nourishment and never feel the sun on my face. Even if I just had the freedom to wander the markets myself, to escape briefly from the prison I lived in, that would be a reprieve I would treasure. "List every flower you can think of," Isha said, interrupting my thoughts.

"I'll try." Wetting my lips, I began. "Jasmine, lotus, marigold, sunflower…"

"There. It's beginning to work. I can see you, but the light goes through you like it would a wandering spirit."

"Magnolia, dahlia, orchid, chrysanthemum…"

"Just a little bit more."

"Lily, rhododendron, amaranth, clematis, Calliandra."

"There now. You are fully visible. How do you feel?"

"I feel fine. I did not sense that I was using magic."

"We will practice while your father is away. You must be able to control this, Bai."

And practice we did. By the time he returned, an all too short four months later, the ability to make myself invisible came easily, but try as we might, I could not transfer or share the gift with Isha. Our happiness in my new talent soon became resignation since I refused to leave my guardian, though she wasted many hours and even more tears in trying to convince me to escape without her. Ultimately, we decided not to risk exposing the gift, and I mostly remained in my room as I had before.

During the next few years, there were only a few rare occasions when I used my newfound ability. One had been to escape the untoward advances of the few of my father's men who dared risk his wrath. Even as a young girl, I'd been subject to their leers and pinches when my father wasn't looking. They warned me that if I told him what they'd done, they would do something horrible to Isha. As I approached womanhood, their threats became more commonplace, and they sought out opportunities to catch me alone.

When one did, I escaped into the next room and willed myself to vanish. Though he suspected I'd tricked him somehow, he dared not tell my father, for then he'd have to explain the reason he'd been in my chamber in the first place.

I used my power a few times after that to spy on the guards or to steal little sweetmeats to give Isha as presents, but she felt that the risk was too great, and to keep her happy, I stopped using my ability unless it was absolutely necessary. Thanks to Isha's vigilance and my gifts, I managed to escape all that meant me harm except for my father. The danger should he discover my abilities was undeniable so I suffered his abuse in silence.

Though I would have liked nothing more at the moment when my father circled me than to vanish, I gave him a tight smile and steeled my resolve. With a swish of my skirts, we were through the door and down the wide hallway, Hajari following silently behind us, which meant he was to act as my personal guard for the evening.

I climbed into the opulent carriage on loan from the king and allowed the air of celebration to swirl around me. There was a spark of excitement that invigorated my senses, and even though I was with my father, the opportunity to see beyond the walls of my living space was so rare that I determined to bask in it and take in every sight and sound. Before I could catch myself, I smiled. My father noticed.

"You look like your mother when we first met."

The smile left my face, and I replaced it with a neutral expression before allowing the curtain to close and turning toward him. "She was beautiful," I said indifferently. It wasn't a question or an invitation to open a dialogue but a flat statement that I knew to be true. I'd long ago found that it was easier and safer only to answer when it was expected and, even then, to say as little as was politely possible. I'd also learned not to create falsehoods that my father could easily unravel.

"Yes. She was," he answered. "But she is"—he leaned forward—"no longer."

I understood his message. He expected men to fawn over me tonight, and my actions would be carefully watched. "I understand, Father," I said and lowered my eyes, clasping my hands lightly in my lap.

After that exchange, he ignored me and conversed with Hajari, who sat entirely too near. Through my many layers of silk, I could feel his thigh pressed against mine, and from time to time, he purposely moved his leg in my direction, nudging me. Trying to disregard him, I slid closer to the window and snuck glances at the passing city.

The whole town was lit up, and as the horses turned the corner, the palace came into view. It was built on a hilltop, giving it a panoramic view of the surrounding city. Beyond the buildings were forests, a wide lake, and hills that offered protection from our king's enemies. The magnificent citadel was built entirely of marble and granite, and with its various towers, cupolas, and balconies, there were plenty of places to explore. Unfortunately I would never have that opportunity.

We sped toward the first of three arched gateways, each named for the carved marble guardians that stood on either side at the base of each arch. The first was the Vanar Pol with two large monkey statues. Then came the Bagh Pol, or The Gate of the Twin Tigers. I shivered when I saw the terrifying set of tiger guardians with teeth and claws bared.

Last was the Hathi Pol, or the Elephant Gate, with a life-sized elephant standing at each end, trunks raised and large tusks jutting forward. Though there were no signs of it, I knew that the wide lot on the other side of the Elephant Gate was used for elephant fights—a new and horrific practice my father had instigated. He claimed that the fighting was used to assess which elephants were the strongest, the most powerful, and the winners were used in his war campaigns.

I knew that he encouraged the contests not to filter out the weak, though that was certainly something he would do, but to stir the blood of the men. The fights were staged, and the beasts were given opium to make them more vicious than normal. The elephant battles attracted the most bloodthirsty of men, vicious warriors with no compassion who sought to profit from war and the pain of others. In short, it was a way to recruit the types of men he wanted to surround himself with.

But for the party, the battles and blood had been scrubbed away. The palace gleamed with thousands of lamps and the colorful dresses of hundreds of women, who, wearing tinkling jewelry, graced the walkways as if they were vibrant flowers bobbing among the scenery.

Inside, the sparkling light reflected off the wall paintings, colored glass, marble, and mirrors. Fantastic murals depicted the great victories of past kings. Each room, each hallway, each open terrace was a masterpiece of architecture, and every corner was filled with the riches of the kingdom—precious vases collected from exotic locations, art that had been completed by masters under commission, and sculptures so beautiful I wanted to run my fingertips over the carved details.

Despite the opulence of the palace interior, there was one thing above all else I wanted to see—the famed raised garden of the uppermost court. I knew my father wouldn't wish to visit such a place. There were no courtiers, no diplomats, no political strategies going on there, but I thought, perhaps, if I could just catch a glimpse of the legendary garden, then I would commit the sight of it to memory and reflect upon it through my long and lonely years.

Unfortunately, I lingered a bit too long by a marble statue of the goddess Durga, and my father jerked my arm painfully and squeezed my wrist until the blood throbbed hotly in my hand. We moved silently ahead until we came across a couple my father wished to speak with.

He finally let go of my wrist, and I twisted my hand back and forth with as little movement as possible until the feeling returned to my fingers. My reprieve was short-lived, though, and we soon entered the king's reception room—a wide area bedecked with so many lanterns and so much greenery that I felt like I was in a forested grove beneath hundreds of stars.

My father led me from person to person, and I couldn't help but notice that nearly every man who approached appeared to be assessing me. One was even bold enough to reach for my veil. Immediately his fingers fell away and he began to choke. Water spilled from his mouth in such vast amounts as to be unnatural. Quickly, he sped away, and I was unsure if the man survived our encounter.

"Come, Yesubai," my father instructed as he took my arm in a tight grip. "I must speak with the king to discover why your presence warrants such…unsolicited interest."

As we waited for our turn to speak to the king, my father's

impatience left bruises on my already sore arm, though from all outward appearances, he seemed unperturbed. Lokesh stared unabashedly at the king's golden throne, his eyes deferential when someone turned to him but calculating when they looked away.

Finally, it was our turn to approach. The old king smiled kindly at me and clapped his hands together in delight.

"Lokesh, the war hero! How fares our army?" the king asked with an expression that clearly showed he was more interested in the celebration than in my father's answer.

Bowing stiffly, my father replied quietly, "Our enemies cower before the power of your throne, Great King."

"Very good," the king said dismissively. "Now then. I suppose you are wondering why I arranged this festival and specifically asked for your daughter to attend."

"I am…curious," Lokesh responded.

"Ah, my genius friend, I am delighted. If I truly have kept this secret from you and all of your palace spies, then I will happily take credit for achieving something most mortal men cannot—deceiving the master of cunning. Fortunate was the day you entered my kingdom, Lokesh."

"I feel exactly the same way, My King."

"Yes."

"Now, perhaps you might be persuaded to share your secret."

The king chuckled. "Yes, my secret. The king clapped my father's shoulder, a gesture I knew my father detested. "My friend, you know that I have no surviving children of my own and that you are the next natural leader in the kingdom."

My father smiled—an oily, snakelike countenance that frightened me to my core. Apparently, it didn't have the same effect on the gullible king. The man sitting on the throne had a jackal in his midst masquerading as a faithful dog. It was only a matter of time before his new pet turned and devoured him.

"You flatter me," Lokesh said.

"Not at all. Any praise I give is well deserved. Now then, I have been carefully studying your activities and forays into other kingdoms."

"Oh?" my father said.

"Quite. I've come to appreciate your efforts to expand the borders of our kingdom through diplomacy, negotiation, or"—he leaned forward and lowered his voice—"intimidation."

More like conspiracy, confrontation, and terrorization, I thought.

The king continued, "As such, I have embarked upon a bargain of my own."

Little shock waves of pain blistered my arm where my father held on to it. I could literally feel the anger pulsing beneath his fingertips.

"What have you done?" My father managed to twist the words to sound carefree, though I sensed the real threat behind them. The king was, of course, oblivious.

Gleefully, he announced, "I have invited some of the most powerful men from the surrounding kingdoms here with the promise that one of them"—the king raised his eyebrows and darted his eyes quickly from side to side—"the one who offers the most pleasing bargain, will have your daughter, the lovely Yesubai, to wife."

exhibition

My breath caught and my body froze. For a panicked moment, I thought I'd vanished, but the king darted his eyes between me and my father, trying to gauge our reactions. Fortunately for me, my veil obscured the shock I managed to quickly hide. The tension in my father's hand did not show at all on his face. He gave the king a taut smile.

"And how long have you been planning this, Great King?" my father inquired politely, though I could tell he was seething. My stomach wrenched painfully, an indication that he was gathering his power around him. I'd never felt it emanating from him with such tremendous force before. I could almost sense the darkness coalescing inside him. It boiled and churned, rising up like a volcano about to erupt. That he could contain it at all surprised me.

"Oh, for at least several weeks. I have to admit, I am pleased with the response. It would seem that the interest of many powerful men has been piqued. I have been quite busy fueling their desire to take to wife the daughter of my practically infamous military advisor. That so many have come is a tribute to our mutual reputation and the inroads you have made in the name of my kingdom, my friend. Not to mention the unabashedly true rumors of your great beauty, my dear."

The king added the last in an attempt to flatter, but instead his words chilled me. I knew nothing would persuade my father to marry me off to anyone, even a man he could conceivably gain from. The fact was, I belonged to him and he had no intention of letting me leave. He'd made that fact very plain to me over the years.

Finally, my father spoke. Giving the king a jackal smile, he said, "How fortunate we are to be of use to the royal house. My daughter would be…honored to meet the suitors you have brought to our kingdom."

I didn't miss the use of "our" when he spoke of the kingdom. Otherwise what he'd said astonished me. When he hadn't found a clever yet polite way to reject the king's offer, I couldn't help but wonder what his strategy was.

Surely, he could have argued that I was too young, that I was the only female to care for the household since the passing of my dear mother, a falsehood that might be easily believed by one as naive as the king, or that the timing was just not right. Even I could come up with a dozen reasons to rationalize a quiet rejection of the king's offer.

Perhaps my father simply didn't wish to embarrass the king. Maybe he'd been caught off guard and hadn't yet come up with an alternative. Risking a glance at the man standing at my side, I could see that he was once again under control. He was playing at being the diplomat as he turned to one man and then another. The rising power I'd sensed had ebbed again, cloaking itself from all but the most discerning.

Though I tried not to allow hope that the king's offer might actually come to fruition to blossom in my heart, it did. Even the vilest of men at the celebration were better options than staying with my father. All it would take was a lapse in security, a small moment of complacency, a fragment of trust, and I would make my escape with Isha. Perhaps this shocking scheme would be my way out.

The king made his announcement immediately, inviting my father and me to stand with him on the dais.

"My friends! Gather around. As you know, I have not been blessed with a child and have no royal successor, but that does not mean that my kingdom is without prized jewels. In fact, my clever and most loyal military advisor has a daughter, indeed one who is lovelier than a goddess, and he has graciously allowed me the opportunity to give her away in marriage much as I would had I a daughter of my own.

"What we seek is a union. A perfect match. She desires to be joined with a proper groom, of course, but this will be a merging not just of people but of nations, of power, and of affluence. Come! Look closer. Her decorum is without blemish. Her innocence and youth would allow a man to mold her into the sort of companion that would best suit him. A more perfect wife you could not aspire to."

The king stood up and circled around me. My father reluctantly let go of my arm. The fact that I was on display was humiliating, but what was worse was the knowledge that my father would somehow blame me for the king's actions. Not only would he beat me severely but there was now no way he would leave the city. Not with my future uncertain.

Enjoying his grandstanding, the king continued with a flourish. Each claim he made stirred the crowd even more. "Truly I have never seen a flower of such beauty. She is as rare a gem as she is precious. I would know as I am one of the privileged few to have seen her without her veil."

At this my father glanced down at me, his eyes glittering like sharp daggers. He had long ago insisted that I keep myself veiled when in public, and I always had. The king had never had an opportunity to see my face. At least I didn't believe he could have. The only place I went without a veil was within my own chamber.

"I must confess, my friend"—the king clapped my father on the back—"I was passing your home and saw your young daughter at the open window, her face aglow with moonlight. I was captivated by her exquisite face."

My heart sank. I was usually so careful to hide myself from the outside world, but when the moon was full a few months ago, I hadn't been able to sleep. It was hot and I crept to my window, allowing the sweet breeze and the cool light of the full moon to bathe my overwarm skin. That was when the king must've seen me.

Now, thanks to the king's confession, I would be moved. There would be no more flowers because there would be no more windows. Isha and I would be housed in a walled-up dungeon of a space without light, without air, without even a glimpse of the outside world.

Dejected, I lent only half an ear to the king. "Though I am an old man," he said, "even I was struck by her great beauty. My military advisor has kept her all to himself over the years, but to hide such a treasure from the world is a disservice. So tonight my gift to you is to allow all of you to partake in the splendor of my palace, enjoy the succulent fruits of my garden, and bask in the perfection of our women."

I didn't know what the king was going to do until he was at my back. Clumsily, he tugged at my veil, pulling it away from my face. The pins were wrenched painfully from my hair, and several long, black strands fell away with the golden veil. I felt naked and exposed, but I stood tall, knowing instinctively that cowering would not be the proper thing to do.

For some reason, my father had allowed this to happen. Maybe it was to teach me a lesson or to put me in my place. Whatever the reason, I felt the inherent need to protect myself, and protection, when it came to my father, meant one thing only. So, I lifted my shoulders, schooled my expression, and lowered my eyes.

The king put his hand beneath my chin and lifted my head. "Let them all see you, my dear."

I gave him a polite smile and looked around at the people staring up at me. There were a few audible gasps, several leering men, and a few women who looked at me with marked jealousy. Others gave me pitying glances or looked me up and down in a cold, calculating way, but whatever the response from each person, there appeared to be not one soul in the room who was not staring at me.

But then I found one. A single man stood in the back studying the statue of the goddess Durga. He had filled a plate and had his back turned to us as he ate, seemingly entirely uninterested in the king's announcement.

The man was young, perhaps only a few years older than myself. He wore a dark coat trimmed in gold that accented his powerful shoulders and narrow waist. His thick, shoulder-length hair curled at the ends, and I was surprised to find that I wanted to see his face. Why would a man come to the celebration and not want to be a part of it? Perhaps he had no interest in taking a bride. When he touched the exact same spot on the goddess's hand that I had earlier, my curiosity was sparked. Who was he?

"There now. Did I not tell you she was beautiful?" the king asked openly.

"Breathtaking," one leering man nearby murmured as he gave me a suggestive smile.

"Quite lovely," an older man added as he came forward and introduced himself to my father and reacquainted himself with the king. The older man seemed kind. Perhaps he was offering himself as a groom.

I'd never allowed myself to entertain the possibility that I would have a chance to wed someone young and handsome—a man who I could love and come to trust. For my purposes, an older man might be the better choice. It would likely be an easier arrangement to escape from. When the older gentleman looked my way, I gave him a shy smile.

My father was busy and didn't see, but Hajari did, and I knew there would be a reckoning later, but perhaps salvation could be bought with a few careful smiles and some feigned interest. When the king formally introduced me to the old sultan, I bravely asked if perhaps he might share a plate of food with me.

He was delighted and offered his arm to escort me to the buffet tables. The king looked on proudly. I didn't dare look at my father. Unfortunately my escort followed closely behind.

"Don't mind my guard, Hajari," I said. "My father dotes on me and ensures my safety."

"Of course. I understand," the well-dressed man replied. As he filled a plate for us, he asked, "Do you think you might enjoy living by the sea?"

"Do you live in Mumbai?" I asked attentively.

"No. I live in Mahabalipuram. Do you know of my city?"

"I confess I do not."

"Our city is bustling with a busy port. We trade with many far-off lands, and we have several artisans and sculptors who make our temples and shrines beautiful. Perhaps you would consider a visit."

"She would not wish to live in a city of coarse sailors, Devanand. She belongs in a city of beauty. Allow me to introduce myself, my lovely. My name is Vikram Pillai."

"Bah, you are a merchant! Your title is purchased. My blood is royal!"

"Your blood is old. She needs a groom who can walk without assistance."

"How dare you! Please disregard his outbursts, my dear. A young girl as innocent and as fresh as you are should not be subjected to such inappropriate disturbances."

"Her youth is the issue at hand. I am a much better match. And I can offer wealth. There is no one else with more profitable trade caravans."

"You might have more wealth at your disposal, but you forget that I have a fleet. An alliance with my kingdom would be a much wiser decision."

"We'll see about that!"

"Yes. Indeed we shall!"

The younger man with a droopy mustache left us alone, and I felt grateful, but he wasn't the first interruption or the last. A circle of men had surrounded us, each one clamoring for attention and offering his wealth, his lands, his titles, or, in some cases, his person, in exchange for my hand in marriage. It was overwhelming. What little I'd been able to pluck from our shared plate soon turned to ash in my mouth. A hand latched on to my arm and tugged me not too gently from the circle of men.

"Gentlemen, my daughter will return momentarily. Please allow me a moment to speak with her in private."

My father's grip on my arm was absolute, and there was a strange expression on his face. There was no doubt he was irritated by the whole situation and found the pawing men distasteful. At the same time, there was something behind his eyes, an unexplained delight that made my blood run cold.

He nodded to a passerby and waited for us to be alone, then said quietly, "The king has graciously"—his words dripped with sarcasm—"invited us to stay the night. You will retire to the women's wing. As soon as the king says his good-nights to his guests, Hajari will escort you as far as the outer doors. You will behave yourself with the proper decorum I expect, and in the morning, I will summon you. If I discover anything, anything at all, in your behavior to be what I would consider inappropriate or not to my liking, Isha will suffer horribly. Do I make myself clear?"

"Yes, Father."

"Good. Now cover your face. The men here have ogled you enough tonight, I should think."

"Of course."

Immediately I worked at reattaching my veil, and when it was done to his satisfaction, he left me alone again with Hajari, who whispered hotly at my ear, "You think this is your chance to leave, but you aren't going anywhere. I see you strutting around like you're the king's prize when we both know you're nothing but a plaything. A broken little doll."

Hajari risked running his hand up my arm. I stiffened but said nothing. "You see, I know what all these other men don't. That you like being knocked around, and someday when your father isn't watching as carefully, I'll show you the proper way to play."

Fortunately, another suitor appeared at that moment and Hajari backed away. The rest of the evening, I was kept busy being escorted on the arm of various men, each attempting to coax my favor in one way or another despite the fact that we all knew the decision rested with the king and my father and not with me. Had I been able to choose, I would likely go with Devanand. The idea that Isha and I could disappear on a ship to a faraway land was appealing.

Through the night, I caught glimpses of the quiet stranger as he wandered the hall. There was no doubt he was a warrior. His powerful build and the way he carried himself made it obvious. Once a servant carrying a tray of sliced fruit stumbled, and he not only caught it but he helped the woman right herself. At that moment, he turned and I sucked in a breath. He was the most handsome man I'd ever seen.

On the arm of Devanand again, I asked carefully, "Who is that young man? The one there dressed in black?"

"Where?"

"The one talking with Vikram Pillai," I murmured quietly.

"Oh, that's the younger Rajaram son."

"Rajaram?" I prompted.

"Yes. His brother is heir to the throne so he wouldn't be a good match for you, if that is what you're thinking. I am not surprised you asked about him though. He is young, and I would think a girl such as yourself would find him attractive."

I quickly patted the Mahabalipuram king's arm and reassured him. "Not at all. I simply haven't been introduced to him yet."

"It is unlikely he will wed before his brother. Perhaps he is here to negotiate a match in his stead."

"It has not come up. Besides, being as young as I am, it might behoove me to be matched with someone with more experience. An older man can help me navigate the troubled waters of youth. Wouldn't you agree?"

He laughed, pleased with my reference to his city, and introduced me to some other men he considered allies.

Finally, the festivities were concluded, and those staying at the palace were escorted to their various chambers to take their rest. Hajari and I trailed behind a servant girl who led us down a series of long halls. It was late and the full moon cast its mellow light over us as we walked. Every few feet, an open archway allowed the soft night breezes to ruffle my skirts.

When we arrived at an elaborately carved double door, the servant bowed and opened it, indicating I should enter. Hajari narrowed his eyes in warning but said nothing. After the doors closed behind me, shutting out the sight of my father's man, I breathed a sigh of relief and followed the servant.

She led me to a spacious chamber with a huge bed. A bath had been drawn, and she stayed long enough to help me. A sleeping gown had been left for me, and after I was made comfortable, the servant departed. I was alone. Truly alone. I didn't know what would happen to me when the sun came up the next morning, but for the moment, I was out of danger.

Unable to sleep though I was exhausted, I rose from my bed and walked out to the balcony. The moon had sunk farther, but I guessed only an hour had passed since I retired. The soft breeze carried the scent of jasmine, and I heard the unmistakable sound of water. A series of steps led upward from my balcony, and I suddenly realized that the king's hanging garden might be just a few steps away.

Glancing around, I willed myself invisible and, with the moon lighting my way, stepped, hidden, into the night.

blush

ollowing the sound of the water, I crept silently up the stairs. Guards were posted on the parapets, but they didn't even glance in my direction. The grit under my feet and the breeze on my bare skin made me feel alive. My pulse quickened as I ascended to the level of the guards. With a little exploration, I found another set of stairs not too far from where the first set ended. On the side of the stairwell, a small waterfall tumbled down the wall from overhead. I knew it must be coming from the hanging garden so I climbed higher.

Now three levels above the sleeping chamber I'd been assigned to, I paused at a wide balcony and looked out over the moonlit city. Most of the lamps had been snuffed out for the evening, but there was enough light remaining from torches, fires, and candles around the buildings in the city that the dark structures below looked like they were lit with fireflies. As beautiful a view as it was, I was after something else.

Quietly making my way around the corridor, I found no other set of stairs. Instead there were several doors. Nervous about testing them, I placed my hand on each and listened quietly before opening them. The first had stairs leading down. The second held various weapons—arrows, bows, shields, and spears. The third door was the heaviest and opened with a loud creak. I froze, hoping no one heard.

When there was no telltale sign of heavy boots headed my way, I slipped inside the darkened doorway and found another set of stairs going up. I hesitated, thinking I might lose my way back, but my desire to see the garden pulled me forward, and I went up one step and another until I emerged at the end of a tunnel. Moonlight and the smell of water and green living things beckoned me forward.

I rushed ahead and stepped through an open archway into paradise. During the day, the gardens must have been breathtaking, but at night, lit only by stars and moonbeams, the garden was magical. Each dark alcove whispered of secrets waiting for me to discover them.

Rumors were that the king had wooed his late bride on the manicured paths while walking among the murmuring foliage. It was easy to picture a courting couple wandering beneath the trees, taking advantage of the enchanting concealment they offered.

Moving deeper into the garden, I noted the thick stone pillars supported tier after tier of greenery that rose above me in steps like a theater. On the left was a multi-leveled terrace threaded through with delicate little vines. On the right was a gallery of living art with arched doorways leading down to other levels.

On each echelon, there were carved statues, trickling fountains, towers of hanging plants, and even living sculptures made of greenery. Though there were no torches to offer light, the rays of the moon penetrated the leafy canopy well enough that I could notice nearly every detail.

A stone walkway appeared to circumnavigate the entire garden. Around it was recently turned soil, dark and nutrient-rich. Crouching down, I pressed my hand into the soft stuff. I couldn't find the stone floor that would support such a weight, but judging from the size of the trees, the largest of which had trunks wider than I was tall, the ceiling holding the garden must be very thick indeed, perhaps twenty feet or more.

In the center of the garden was a massive fountain of such magnificence I spent the better part of an hour running my hands over the carved figures and through the water. Curious, I followed the path of the streams. It appeared that a series of aqueducts brought water to the roof of the citadel using dozens of cisterns that carried the water up from the river.

All the levels were built at a slight angle, which allowed the water to flow downhill, irrigating the entire garden. What wasn't used in the garden was directed back to the river when it spilled over the side of the building in a waterfall. The design was genius.

Huge shade trees soared high above the building walls, and it gave me the sense of being at the top of a very great mountain. I examined the tender new growth of tiny plants wet with evening dew, plucked a tiny budding flower and tucked it behind my ear, and admired a section of new plantings the garden cultivator had just put in.

The warm night breeze lifted the leaves on the trees, making them dance and sigh as if they were alive. The sound of it teased my senses. I walked through a multi-level maze only to emerge in a grove of perfect fruit trees full of ripening spheres of all descriptions.

Beyond that was a small, evergreen meadow—the lush grass a perfect place for taking a picnic lunch. How romantic it would be to dine there under the shadow of a tree with the murmuring of the fountain and the view of the city. I lay on the grass with my hands behind my head and stared up at the countless constellations filling the night sky, thinking that if I was incredibly lucky, I might be soon looking at the same view from the deck of a ship taking me and Isha to another land.

Wanting to explore more, I left the soft blades of grass and continued on. Flowers seemed to spring from every spare patch of ground. I plucked an orange marigold and tossed it into the stream of water, laughing softly as I followed it. The small flower danced and bobbed until I came to the edge of the garden where it tumbled over the wall and disappeared.

This part of the garden was on level with the circuit wall, and I had a clear view of the citadel's battlements and the soldiers who stood on guard. Not wanting to leave but knowing I should make my way back to my bed, I slowly wound up the levels, taking in every sight, scent, and sound. Reluctant to continue on, I stopped at the central fountain once again and discovered a water plant I'd never seen before.

It looked like a lotus blossom, but instead of the common pink or white color, the flower had lavender hues. It was the loveliest thing I'd ever seen. Tempted to pluck it from the water yet knowing if my father found it in my room he'd know what I'd been up to, I instead examined it from all angles, committing it to memory.

So intent was I in my study that I didn't hear footsteps until the person approaching was almost directly behind me. I froze and looked down at my arm, letting out a little sigh of relief that I was still invisible. Still, the person came closer and only stopped just short of running into me. Biting my lip, I took a careful step away, wincing as my foot knocked a small pebble.

Quickly looking up, I found myself staring into the golden eyes of the man I'd noticed earlier at the party, the one seemingly disinterested in the king's announcement regarding my eligibility for marriage. His eyes narrowed as he looked down at the place where the small stone had rolled, and then he scanned the trees surrounding us. After a moment, he let out a small sigh and placed both hands on the rim of the fountain.

He stared into the water as if he were trying to divine his future and didn't seem to like what he saw. Then he noticed the purple flower I'd recently dropped, scooped it up into his hands, and brought it to his face. He inhaled deeply and sighed. I found the scent of the man standing next to me more intoxicating than that of the flower. Unlike the other men downstairs who carried with them the scent of the alcohol they had drunk or the garlic they had eaten, this man smelled of musky sandalwood and the scent of sweet grass warmed by the sun.

Satisfied, he gently dropped the water flower back down into the fountain, where it turned in a lazy circle before floating back. It was as if there was something magnetic about the man that drew the exceptional blossom toward him. Suddenly, I realized that I, too, had come dangerously close to touching him.

Leaning back at an awkward angle, so he wouldn't sense me, I wondered how long he would be standing in my very personal space. When he didn't immediately move, I studied him in much the same way as I did the garden. The fact that he was handsome was obvious, but I'd been around handsome men before and had always remained largely unaffected. A handsome man could be just as cruel as an ugly one. I'd had far too many uncomfortable experiences with men to simply trust one based on his appearance.

That he was an emperor's son meant he was powerful, but he didn't wear his power in an obvious way like my father did. That fact made me like him more. His clothing was well made but didn't boast the typical trappings that declared to everyone that a rich man wore them. His body was that of a warrior, not a king, which likely meant his father was still alive and, what was more, it meant that he was brave—a man who stood alongside his soldiers rather than behind them.

His features were not typical of the men I'd come across before. The shape of his face and mouth seemed different somehow, and his golden eyes, with little streaks of rust the color of newly made henna ink, were so uncommon as to be remarkable. He was as exotic and rare as the flower I'd just come across—a bewitching, transfixing contradiction of a man.

He was a soldier and yet he seemed to have an appreciation for things of beauty. An heir to a large empire and yet here he was alone, without a bodyguard or an entourage. No one was about to scrape at his feet or offer obeisance. Here was an entitled, attractive prince who seemingly cared nothing for parties, diplomacy, or eligible females. And where most men would strike the help for being careless, he was not only kind but assisted the servant—a gesture few men I knew would make, especially for one they considered beneath their station.

As I watched him twitch his fingers above the koi pond, I smiled and had to stop myself from laughing at the hungry little fish lifting their heads above water and making supplicating shapes with their mouths. They were hungry and sought the sustenance they thought he might provide.

"I'm sorry. I didn't bring you any bread," he said. "If I knew you were here, I would have."

My amusement was replaced by something else, something warm, a feeling I couldn't quite describe. Heat colored my cheeks, and I silently pressed my hands against them. Amazed, I realized I was blushing from just being in his presence. My pulse quickened as I stared at his face as hungrily as the colorful fish. In fact, I couldn't seem to look away from him until I noticed his brow furrow in confusion, and he glanced in my direction.

"What is it?" he asked. "What ethereal creature have you discovered?"

I looked down at the bobbing school only to cup my mouth in horror when I realized that the fish had given up on the handsome young man and were now turned in my direction. They saw through whatever spell it was that made me invisible to others. As their wide mouths opened and closed and they swam closer, he took a step in my direction. Just at that moment, a man called out.

"There you are. Thank you for agreeing to see me."

The young prince stopped; his whole body stiffened as he turned to acknowledge the newcomer. Stepping into the clearing around the fountain, the man strode confidently forward, the mask he wore a version of his earlier self. Younger than the wizened diplomat my father typically preferred—this one he only wore when he met with those much younger than he was.

It wasn't different enough that most people would notice. In fact, I appeared to be the only one who saw my father for what he truly was—a decrepit, skeletal corpse—a man as decayed on the outside as he was rotted on the inside. What could he possibly want with this young man? I wondered. Despite the fact that my every instinct told me to run away as quickly as possible, another part of me wanted to stay, wanted to stand between the handsome stranger and my father and protect him as I did Isha.

The young man answered. "Your…summons didn't give me leave to deny your request."

"And why would you? I assure you that this dialogue will be of vital importance to the future of both of our kingdoms." My father smiled in a charming way that rooted me to the spot where I stood. "Perhaps you will allow me to introduce myself properly." He bowed and held out his hand in a gesture of goodwill. "My name is Lokesh."

The young man ignored the offered hand. "I know who you are."

"Ah, I can see that my reputation precedes me."

"Indeed it does. Though I hope it is exaggerated, my impression is that it is not."

My father clucked his tongue. "Surely a warrior such as yourself knows that a sometimes admittedly shocking reputation can often serve to benefit its wielder just as much, if not perhaps more, than a finely made sword?"

Folding his arms across his brawny chest, the stranger answered, "Yes. And I also know that the type of man willing to allow such a reputation to exist, whether it is true or not, is a man I would not have at my back."

Lokesh laughed in response. I'd never heard him laugh before, even facetiously, and as far as I could tell, his reaction was genuine. For some reason, the stranger's answer delighted my father. The nervous feeling I had regarding the safety of the young man intensified by several degrees.

"How clever. But, then again, I would expect no less of a Rajaram."

The young man's eyes narrowed. "I sense that my time here has been wasted. We had been informed that this meeting would be regarding treaty negotiations. Instead, I find myself a guest at a women's garden party where I am forced to watch pompous peacocks strut around in all their finery as they flatter, preen, and prance around, congratulating one another on the amount of gold stored in their coffers. The hour grows late, and as my intention is to leave with the sunrise, I would prefer to retire to my bedchamber for the few hours remaining until that time. If it is the recent skirmish you wish to discuss, then I would suggest you get on with it. If not, I will take my leave."

Lokesh's eyes sparkled. "Kishan. May I call you that?" My father didn't wait for approval but continued. "I can assure you that the recent"—he paused—"small scuffles between our troops, as trivial as they are, have indeed been on my mind. The fact that our two realms have been set at odds pains me, and I feel I must attempt to persuade you that I have in no way been the instigator of such treacherous acts."

The stranger said nothing, but his fists tightened, and the muscles in his arms flexed. He clearly didn't believe the lies spilling from my father's lips, at least not completely. I wasn't sure what it was Lokesh had been doing in all of his secret campaigns, but it was now clear that he had malicious aims regarding this young man and his family. The fear I felt for him almost choked me. My body shook and my breathing became ragged.

"No, Kishan. My purpose tonight is to put an end to any discontent and build a bridge between our people."

"And how do you propose we do that?" the stranger asked.

Taking a step forward and raising his hand in such a way as to appear supplicating to the outsider, but was obviously threatening from my perspective, he said, "By creating an alliance between our families."

4

bait

I couldn't help it and let out a soft, involuntary gasp. Fortunately, neither my father nor the young man noticed it over the sounds of the flowing fountain.

"What do you mean?" the handsome man asked. He was right to be suspicious. Whatever my father was planning would not bode well for anyone involved.

Lokesh turned and approached the water fountain. Allowing the stream to run over his fingertips, he queried, "You are, of course, aware of the king's announcement tonight?"

"That your daughter is now eligible for marriage? What of it?"

A part of me was hurt by the young man's remark. I rationalized it by reminding myself that I wasn't looking for a suitor anyway. That the best thing for me and Isha was if I married a man who lived far away from my father. Far enough away that I could escape. Such a thing would be easy with the King from Mahabalipuram, but I suspected that leaving a man like this stranger would prove far more difficult. Still, to hear of his indifference to me was a blow to my feminine pride.

I'd always known that I was beautiful. Isha told me as much daily, and I'd garnered enough attention from the men surrounding our home as to be confident in my appearance, but for the first time in my life, I felt…unappealing. The idea that the young man that I found so very fascinating had no interest in me whatsoever stung.

My father went on. "You may be unaware of this, but the announcement tonight was unplanned. The king intends to use my daughter to further his reach, and as she is the only connection I have remaining to my beloved, late wife, you may understand that the declaration regarding her eligibility for marriage has caused me some concern."

I narrowed my eyes at the mention of my mother. Isha had shared her suspicions regarding my mother's death long ago. She told me that my mother didn't die in childbirth as my father led everyone to believe. Her friend, the midwife who delivered me, had spoken to Isha just hours after I was born and reported that both mother and daughter were healthy.

When Isha's friend went back to check on me and my mother, my mother's death was announced and the midwife disappeared. Isha believed wholeheartedly that my father had both women disposed of. Having seen his temper firsthand, I didn't doubt he was capable of the feat. If I thought killing him was a possibility, I would have done it myself, long ago. The handsome man spoke, distracting me from my thoughts of revenge.

"What does this have to do with me?" the stranger asked.

My father ran his fingertips back and forth in the water, and I noticed that all the fish disappeared. No longer supplicating, they quickly retreated to the far reaches of the pond. Had they sensed something when my father touched the water? I wondered. Or perhaps he used his power somehow to make them retreat. I bit my lip, so intent on the next words my father uttered that I could barely breathe.

"I thought we might come to a mutually beneficial arrangement."

"Such as?"

"Your elder brother, Dhiren, is it? I have heard that he has not as yet taken a bride."

"He's still young. Besides, he's been too busy defending our lands from your…small skirmishes."

My father glanced briefly at the stranger, his lips curved slightly at the man's remark. "Wouldn't it be better," Lokesh asked with a wily smile, "if your brother could return to his duties at home? Forget war and disputes over territory and settle down to be the emperor he is destined to become? With the proper queen at his side, he could take his rightful place. Sire sons to reign in his stead."

"Let me guess. You'd want your daughter to be the queen."

"She is beautiful. Obedient. Demure. What's more, her dowry is backed by the king." He leaned forward and lowered his voice. "And, just between the two of us, with my daughter on the throne, I would be satisfied that my grandchildren would someday rule both kingdoms. The meaningless squabbles over territory would cease, and both of our kingdoms could flourish in a mutually satisfactory way."

The young man rubbed his jaw, and I heard the scrape of stubble on his cheek. I wanted to shout, to scream at him not to heed my father's words. That Lokesh never kept his promises. That even staying here listening to him was dangerous. But I said nothing and wrung my invisible hands, desperate to hear about this future he planned for me. The fact that Lokesh wouldn't allow the king to marry me off to someone of his choosing wasn't surprising, but I'd allowed a small sliver of hope to grow, and as I'd expected, my father had snuffed it out before even an evening had passed.

Then my devious parent added, "Surely, at that point you might be freed to pursue your own goals. Perhaps you can find a wife with enough riches to enable you to purchase a small freehold of your own. Obviously, as the second son, you would be given a portion of your father's wealth to establish yourself. With enough of a start, you might even do well. You'd never be able to keep up with your brother, of course, but there's no shame in being second best. And I'm sure my daughter's royal children would enjoy meeting their uncle should he deign to visit from time to time."

As Lokesh continued, the young man's back straightened even more. His fury was obvious. I knew it and my father knew it. Manipulation was one of his skills, and the only way to circumvent it was to pretend that nothing he said affected you. Again, I found that I wanted to rise to the young man's defense, but there wasn't anything I could do. My father had maneuvered his layers of manipulation around the man as deftly as a snake, and I could almost hear the sound of the handsome stranger's ego being bruised as the coils tightened.

"You understand that I feel a great fatherly affection toward my daughter. It is imperative to me that I keep her close by. Our lands border each other. Because of that, I am willing to negotiate a betrothal on behalf of our king, but make no mistake, should my generous offer be rejected, I will have no choice but to escalate the hostilities between our peoples."

"And you feel comfortable housing your daughter with your so-called enemies?"

Lokesh's tongue darted over his lips. "I have every confidence that you will treat her with the honor and respect she deserves."

I could have laughed. There was no enemy more dangerous to my well-being than the very man who professed to feel "fatherly affection" for me.

The young man called Kishan turned his back to my father, which meant he was facing me. In fact, he was only a few inches away. A myriad of emotions crossed his face as he considered my father's words. I wanted to reach up and stroke the tip of my finger across his brow, to smooth out the wrinkles and ease the discomfort my father had caused him. Finally, he said, "I will pass along your proposal to my parents. We will send our reply by courier within a fortnight."

My father lowered his head in a gesture of feigned good will. "May your horses be swift."

Kishan took his leave then and Lokesh watched him go. Silence descended on the garden. Every creeping thing was still. Even the wind had died down. My breathing suddenly seemed too loud. I swiped at my overheated brow and willed my invisible legs to stop aching. Raising his hands, Lokesh channeled his power, an act I'd rarely witnessed. The water in the fountain snapped and froze as hoary ice soon covered every inch of the path's stony surface.

He whipped his arms in the air, and a stiff wind tore through the garden, ripping delicate flowers from their stems and breaking limbs from the trees. Then he lifted his arms and the ground shook, the frozen fountain cracked, and I stumbled and fell. I bit my tongue hard rather than cry out. Thrusting out his open hands, blue sparks shot from his fingertips and blackened the trunk of a nearby tree. Clenching his fists, he snuffed the power out, and with a determined stride, he left the garden, heading down a different set of steps than the ones I'd used.

I waited a long time before heading back to my sleeping chamber, and once I did, I carefully washed my feet and climbed into bed, but sleep eluded me. Instead, I stared at the filmy material draped over my bed and prepared myself for the morning to come.

When daylight found my chamber, I waited for my father to

come collect me. I'd expected him to appear immediately, but as the morning hours passed and not even a maid came to my chamber, I ventured out. I didn't find anyone, guest or servant, until I entered the great hall, and when I did, the one who sought me out was not my father nor his right-hand man, Hajari, but King Devanand, my would-be suitor from Mahabalipuram.

"Oh, my dear. This is tragic. Tragic news indeed."

"What is it?" I asked him as I adjusted the veil more tightly about my face. "What has happened?"

"Have you not heard?"

I shook my head in response.

"The king has been murdered."

"Is…is it possible?" I asked, suspicion already filling my mind. "How did he die? Was the villain discovered?"

"Not as yet. Your father is investigating."

"I see."

"At first, it was believed he simply expired in his sleep, but as the women tended to him, his nightshirt fell open. That's when they saw the black marks on his chest near his heart."

"Black marks?"

"Yes. The area surrounding his heart was burned, but the blackened skin was not enough to kill him. Still, it is enough proof to raise suspicion."

"I see. What is happening now? Where is my father?"

"He is organizing the troops. They are to defend the kingdom until such time as a new king has been established. He worries that a usurper may try to take the throne, and he does not wish that to happen."

"Of course."

He patted my hand. "Unfortunately, this means there will be no plans made at this time regarding your future. You should know, though, that I have made my intentions very clear to your father. He assured me that I would be among the first to know when everything settles down. Until that time, all the guests are to return as quietly as possible to their own domains."

"I understand."

"Ah. There's your father's man. I'll leave you in his care then. Until we meet again, lovely lady."

The king squeezed my hand and reluctantly gave me over to Hajari, who took my arm in a bruising grip. "Where have you been?" he hissed in my ear.

"No one came to collect me this morning," I replied coldly.

"Your father is waiting for you. Come."

He dragged me down the hall and through several passageways, relishing the opportunity to show me he was in charge, though both of us knew it was only temporary. Sure enough, his demeanor entirely changed the moment we entered the room where my father sat surrounded by the late king's advisors. When he saw me, he dismissed the group.

"Did you sleep well, my dear?" he inquired politely as the last of the men left and closed the door behind them.

"Yes, Father," I answered with my gaze trained on his feet.

"I suppose you heard of the king's demise," he said, and from his tone, I couldn't tell if he meant it as a question or a statement. I decided it was best to say nothing.

He waited for a few seconds and then confirmed what I already suspected. "Tragic, isn't it? Of course, you are aware of what this might mean for you."

"That I'm not to be married after all?" I ventured quietly.

"Oh, you will be married, Yesubai, but not to the geriatric king you so obviously prefer." He turned away and strode back to the king's table, where a large map was spread out. He picked up a figurine of a warrior on the back of an elephant and moved it to another location across a heavy black line drawn upon the map. The territory was marked with the word Rajaram. I glanced away before he looked up at me again.

"You should be happy," he said. "My intention is that you marry someone much younger. And then, once you are a queen and a little time has passed, I'll expect you to kill him." Startled, I looked up and found him peering at me, a devilish gleam in his eye. "To see that you fulfil your part in this little drama, I'll be keeping Isha within arm's length. Do you understand my expectations?" he finished.

After I blinked the moisture from my eyes, I nodded slightly and answered, "Yes, Father."

"Very good. You may leave. We will be residing here until the proper arrangements are made for your betrothal."

It took all of a month for my father to reluctantly ascend to the throne. He kept Isha away from me to insure my compliance. The maids assigned to me were efficient but cold, and Hajari became a constant at my side. Not once did he let me out of his sight. My room was considered too easy to escape and new quarters were assigned to me. There was only one door in and out of my new chamber, and since the dignitaries had all been sent packing, my father was content to leave me there.

My meals were brought in, and I was permitted one walk of the grounds per day and that was only if Hajari was with me. Since I knew being alone with Hajari would only result in a probable assault on my person, I determined that staying in my room was preferable. Without Isha, the only friendly face in my very limited world, I despaired. Food lost its appeal, and I kept the heavy curtains drawn over my barred window.

Then an invitation arrived. The Rajaram family had considered my father's offer despite the unveiled threats behind it, and the queen herself said she would like to meet me to ascertain if I would be a good match for her son. My father was thrilled at the prospect. He had been distracted with the duties of running the kingdom, but when the courier arrived, he couldn't wait to share the news and had me brought to him immediately. He wasn't pleased with my appearance.

"Have you been ill?" he questioned.

"No, Father."

Roughly, he yanked the veil away from my face and narrowed his eyes as he cupped my chin, turning my head one way and another to study me. Shoving me aside, he cornered Hajari and wrapped a hand around the man's throat. His eyes bulged, and he wheezed as he scratched feebly at my father's hand. "You will see to it that she eats, that her hair is brushed and oiled until it shines, and that there is not a mark on her face, or puffiness under her eyes. Have I made myself clear?"

"Yes, my King," Hajari coughed out.

"Good." He let his servant down and added, "She leaves in three days. See to it she's ready. I want her adorned as a princess. Now, go. I must speak to her alone."

Hajari, whose throat was now swollen and red, retreated without a word and shut the door behind him.

My father said, "Now then. There are a few things I think we should discuss before you leave."

Dread filled me when the palace of the Rajaram family came into view. I was in the middle of a large caravan, riding in an opulent carriage, and I was dressed as if I were a great queen already. My father had spared no expense in presenting his deadly little gift to the Rajaram family. Inside a trunk full of sumptuous silk dresses and veils was a hidden compartment packed with bottles of poison and sharpened knives small enough to slip inside a pocket.

I knew the consequences should I fail. My father had made it perfectly clear to me. I was to please Dhiren, the eldest, marry him, discover the secret whereabouts of his family heirlooms, steal them, and kill him. Until that time, I was to spy on the Rajaram family.

If I didn't do what my father wanted, he would torture Isha. I twisted the little lock of Isha's grey hair in my pocket. He'd given it to me as a reminder that I needed to fulfill my duty. In fact, he'd been so specific about the methods he'd use to hurt my nursemaid that I had no doubt that he'd not only done it before but would relish the opportunity to do so again.

My stomach clenched painfully, knowing that I had agreed to become a secret assassin and a spy for the sick, depraved man my father was, but the consequences should I fail were unthinkable. I couldn't allow my beloved Isha to suffer at his hands. I didn't know if I could commit murder to save her, but there was no doubt I owed her for protecting me from him. Every time I saw her, the limp she had reminded me that it was my fault she suffered, my fault she stayed in his employ. I wouldn't leave her in his hands.

When we arrived at the palace, I was introduced, and each person I met seemed open and kind. Hajari had come with me and tried to insert himself as my so-called protector, but thankfully the military advisor, a shrewd man who seemed to see right through my veil to the secrets hidden within my heart, assigned his own man as well. He was wise to do so. Hajari's actions were severely curtailed with a Rajaram soldier constantly nearby.

I didn't meet Deschen until dinner that evening. The queen was the epitome of poise. She watched me from the other side of the table and asked polite questions about my home and family. She interpreted my guarded answers as a case of my being shy. After dinner she called me to her private chamber and bade me sit at her side. Women of all ages surrounded her and chatted happily while they sewed.

When she saw I was reluctant to talk about myself, she spoke of her distant family, of her homeland, and of her sons. Her love for her family was obvious, as was the fact that she was fiercely protective of her children. She seemed surprised when I asked about her younger son but was very willing to share stories of his youth. I soon learned that Kishan had been sent out to the borderlands and would likely return within the month and that Dhiren wasn't expected for some time. Deschen said she wanted to get to know me first before the decision regarding a betrothal would be made.

Every day I was given leave to wander the palace grounds, always with my two escorts, and every evening I spent with Deschen. It didn't take long for me to admire Kishan's mother. She fascinated me almost as much as her son did. It was clear that there was a great love between Deschen and her husband. When it was time to retire, the emperor came to fetch his wife. Together they bid good night to all the widowed women she'd taken in.

The women, whose husbands had died in the war, were fiercely loyal to the Rajaram family, and I felt buoyed by just hearing their stories. I wondered if there might be a way to save Isha. She would flourish as one of the queen's women. I was just beginning to feel at home and safe when my father paid me a visit.

A desperate nightmare woke me. My arms prickled with gooseflesh, and I noticed that the shutters were open, the curtains billowing in the breeze. I'd just gotten up to close them when I heard a voice. "You look well, my dear."

Freezing in place, I instinctively lowered my head. "Father," I said.

"How are things progressing? Has the family accepted you?"

"I believe they have."

"Then what is taking so long? Why have I heard nothing about a betrothal?"

"The queen is still considering me. Besides, both princes are away."

"Yes. I'm keeping them busy."

"But why? I thought we wanted them here."

He moved so quickly I wasn't prepared. My father thrust me up against the wall with his forearm at my throat. "What did you say?" he asked, his dark eyes glittering in the moonlight.

"I apologize," I whispered. "I didn't mean to question you."

"Remember your place," he hissed.

I nodded, cursing myself for being so reckless. My time away from my father had made me complacent.

"I don't need to explain my actions to you. Still, should the queen mention the skirmishes keeping her sons away, you may assure her that you have enough influence over your father to stop them should they agree to the uniting of our families. Have you seen the medallions I asked you to find?"

"No. Neither the queen nor the king wears them on their person. The military advisor does not allow me or Hajari to move about the grounds without one of his men present."

My father muttered, "I should have had that Kadam killed." When I said nothing, he took a step back, finally releasing me from his hold on my neck, and said, "Do you know the reason I seek those medallions?"

"No," I answered carefully. "I only need to know that you want them."

"That is right." He seemed pleased with my answer. Tilting his head, he considered me for a moment, then said, "Perhaps, my dear Yesubai, it is time for you to understand exactly who you are."

I felt the oxygen leave my lungs. "What do you mean?"

"Yes. If you know my motivations, you'll understand how best to serve me." Turning, he clasped his hands behind his back and began. "You are the daughter of a very powerful man, and I don't mean politically." He strolled around the room fingering various objects that belonged to the royal family as he did so. "I was once the heir to a throne of a large province in a land far away from here." He turned back to me. "Even though I had to kill my brother and my step-mother to ascend to the throne, I gave it up."

That he'd killed to accomplish his goals wasn't surprising, but walking away from a throne was. "You didn't want that power?" I questioned.

"Ruling a kingdom isn't power," he spat as he looked down his nose at me. "This is real power." He pulled a chain around his neck and showed me a broken amulet attached to the end.

"What is it?"

"It is called the Damon Amulet."

"Is that a tiger?"

"How very clever of you, my dear." He rubbed his thumb over the amulet with an almost affectionate expression. He murmured quietly, as if lost in thought, "A very long time ago there was a great battle that united the kingdoms of Asia. A demon had appeared. He ravaged the countryside, and finally his atrocities became too horrible to be ignored. Five kingdoms gathered to defeat the monster once and for all."

My father had never told me anything about his past. Most of what I knew I'd gleaned from bits and pieces I'd overheard. I was fascinated and horrified at the same time.

He continued, "On the eve of their defeat, a goddess beautiful and horrible rode in to lead them on her tiger, named Damon." Smiling secretively, he tapped the tiger claws on the medallion.

"When the demon was finally dead, she gifted each kingdom with a piece of the amulet. Soon it was discovered that the amulet pieces controlled the elements—each segment governing one. It is said that if the amulet is ever reassembled, its bearer will wield the power of the goddess herself."

It explained so much—the blue fire I'd seen at his fingertips, the water spilling from the mouth of the man who'd dared touch me, the small tremors in the ground whenever he was angry, the fierce winds he'd summoned in the garden, and the untimely death of the king. This was what drove my father. This was what he sought. And somehow, a portion of this power he'd gathered had been passed on through his blood. My abilities were gifts from a goddess.

He smiled as if taunting a child with a toy. "You can see there are two missing pieces."

"These are the pieces I'm looking for?"

"Yes. Once the amulet is made whole, there won't be anything or anyone I can't control. I will be invincible. And if you're very lucky, you'll live to bask in my glory. It won't be the same as if you were a son, but I never close myself off to new…opportunities." He cupped my chin in his hand, his grip tight. "If only you had a bit of fire in your blood."

A son? Who would he…? Deschen. She was the woman he lusted for.

"But Deschen might be past her childbearing years."

"Yes. That is a possibility," he admitted. "This is why I'm entertaining the notion of allowing you to marry one of the princes. If I cannot have a son to mold in my image, perhaps a grandson will do."

The idea that my father could become even more powerful was astonishing. Everything made sense. The reason I'd been sent. The skirmishes with the Rajaram family. It was all to get those amulets and to wrest Deschen from her family.

Now that I knew my father's true motivation, it was even more imperative that I hide my abilities. If he knew what I could do, he'd mold me and my progeny into what he was—a murderous, power-hungry, vessel of evil. The weaker and more docile I appeared to be, the less he would see me, and the less he saw, the less villainy he'd expect me to participate in.

"You know what I expect," he said. "You have two weeks to either announce your betrothal or find those medallions. For every day after that, I will send you one of Isha's fingers in a box."

Swallowing my horror, my eyes filling with frustrated tears, I murmured, "Yes, Father."

When I looked up, he was gone.

betrothed

Sleep eluded me for the remainder of the night. That my father could gain access to the palace grounds so easily frightened me more than I liked to admit. I despaired, thinking that I would never truly gain any semblance of freedom, that my father's shadow would haunt me and those around me for the rest of my life.

Still, knowing that he had gone to such lengths to insert me into the Rajaram household meant there must be a limit to what he could do. The fact that he needed me to accomplish his purpose was an indication that he wasn't all-powerful. Perhaps, if I was very careful, and very clever, there might be a way to circumvent his plans, but such a betrayal would come with a high price. If I was to move against him, I needed to be absolutely certain of success.

By the time the sun rose, I was dressed and sought out Deschen. Despite the short time I'd been around her, I sensed that she could be trusted, and if there was one thing I needed to beat my father at his own game, it was a powerful ally.

I was told that Deschen was in her women's room and entered without knocking only to find the queen wrapped in the arms of her husband. Of course, I knew I should have left immediately, but my feet were rooted to the spot.

The emperor was a handsome man, much like his son, Kishan, the man I'd been thinking of for weeks despite my determination not to. Deschen's husband wore his power like a mantle across his shoulders, and yet he held his wife as tenderly as if she were a precious flower.

She obviously didn't fear him in any way. In fact, she boldly wriggled away when she noticed me and appeared to fear no reprisal whatsoever in rejecting him. Her husband laughed, not at all angry when she pummeled her fists against his chest, and he seemed not even remotely embarrassed to be caught passionately embracing his wife. He moved behind her, wrapped his arms around her waist, and politely asked if I'd slept well.

Though I opened my mouth to reply, no words came to me, and Deschen rescued me from the awkward situation by reminding him that I was shy, especially around men, and that he should cease from making me uncomfortable and go and find something kingly to do.

"Yes, Hridaya Patni," he answered affectionately.

Chuckling, he gave me a wink, kissed his wife on the cheek, and whispered something in her ear, making her smile, before leaving the room.

When he was gone and she'd made herself comfortable in her favorite chair, she beckoned me closer. Before I'd even taken a step, I blurted, "You love him," almost as an accusation.

"Yes." She smiled and lifted her hand to me. "Is that so shocking?"

I took a few hesitant steps forward. "Men are…"

"Men are…what?" She took my hand and gently pulled me down to a pillow near her feet.

I wrung my hands, wondering how I could finish the sentence without offending her. Finally, I said, "Men are not to be trusted."

She laughed softly and then sobered as she studied my expression. Reaching to the side of my head, she raised her eyebrows, asking my permission. At my nod, she carefully detached the veil covering my face and cupped my chin. The gesture was kind and motherly, and though I tried to contain my emotions, tears filled my eyes. For a long minute, she looked at me. "Has a man hurt you, Yesubai?"

My body shook with little tremors, and when the words eluded me, she said, "Tell me."

I knew that I needed to consider every word as if each one would lead to my death and, what was worse, to Isha's death, but being in her presence made me feel as if hope was a thing I could reach for, as if there might be a happy ending somehow for me. I licked my lips and began to speak, and so intent was our conversation that an hour passed before I paused.

She listened with the kind of empathy I'd only experienced with Isha. When I was done, she stroked my hair and said, "You will be safe with us, Yesubai. I promise you that my son would never treat you unkindly. He will be patient with you. However, if you wish not to wed at this time, you are welcome to stay regardless. I would offer you sanctuary as I do my women. But I hope that you will consider at least meeting my son before you decide."

It was so easy. The kindness she showed made me feel all the more vile, all the more duplicitous, for the things I hadn't shared with her. If anything was sure, I wasn't worthy to be a member of this family. They were trusting, genuine, and without guile. My father would destroy them, and if I couldn't do anything to stop it, I would hold myself accountable for their demise.

After I assured her that it was indeed my intention to ally

myself with her family, she uncovered a hidden doorway behind a curtain, saying that I could use it when I needed to escape Hajari's attention. It led out into the garden, and as I made my way down the secret passage, I willed myself invisible and wondered if I had made a grave error.

My father would be angry at my methods, but even he couldn't deny the results. There was, of course, the possibility that he would never find out. Rajaram's wife had agreed to hold my confession in the strictest of confidence. Still, I thought the potential benefits outweighed the risk.

In order to garner Deschen's sympathy, I'd told her of my father's abuse. Not everything. If I had tried to do that, it would have taken much longer than an hour. In actuality, I'd shared not even of fraction of what I'd experienced at his hands. I didn't disclose his sorcerer-like powers or the fact that he'd threatened Isha's life. I made no mention of the poison secreted in my closet or the knives that fit into concealed pockets sewn into my gowns.

All it took to make her my champion was to speak of my father's anger. I told her about the time he'd destroyed the nursery in a fit of rage over my crying as a baby. That he had beaten Isha senseless for allowing me to make such a noise. Deschen's eyes filled with tears along with mine when I described him throwing me against the wall so hard that it knocked me unconscious. She gasped when I spoke of the months I'd spent locked away from the world with only the flowers to brighten my room.

There were enough stories to tell—tales not so uncommon to women—that I had plenty to share without going into any detail of the supernatural. I added that Hajari had also threatened me multiple times, making inappropriate advances, pinching and touching me when my father wasn't nearby.

Finishing, I begged her not to mention Hajari's abuse or do

anything about it so my father wouldn't know. She agreed but insisted on telling me about the secret passages in the palace. Then she surprised me by saying she thought I would be a good match for her son and that, if I was willing, she'd like to arrange a meeting.

The fact that she accepted me so readily left me feeling skeptical of her abilities to discern. I'd gotten the result I wanted, but I wondered what the cost would be and not just for me but what it would mean for her and her family.

My father returned at the two-week mark, and I gave him the news that Deschen had agreed to the match and wanted to arrange a meeting with Dhiren as soon as a lull in his duties permitted. The news pleased my father. He assured me that the skirmishes would immediately halt so that I might be introduced to my future fiancé.

When I inquired as to Isha's health, he merely gave me a wide smile akin to a cat that's cornered a mouse. Then he whispered more threats, saying that Hajari had been frustrated with my constant disappearances.

I answered with a partial truth. "Hajari makes some of the women here nervous. Deschen has banished him from the women's room, and as I have been garnering her favor, I have been by her side almost continually."

He stared me down as if trying to pick apart the secret thoughts in my head, but finally relented. "Very well. In his free time, I'll have him spy on that Kadam."

Lokesh left by whatever secret means he had come with a promise that he would visit me again, very soon.

The next day, I was sitting near Deschen half listening to the morning reports from the men she sent out to bring her news of the warfront, when one of them said something that perked up my ears.

As he bowed and left, I asked Deschen, "Was he indicating that your son has returned home?"

"Yes." She beamed and then added. "Oh, not Dhiren though. It's my younger son, Kishan, who has returned. I would imagine he will be joining us for our evening meal."

"Oh."

"Do not be concerned. You will meet Dhiren soon enough."

I shook my head and gave her a small smile. "I look forward to it."

"Very good. Now perhaps you will excuse me? I'd like to ensure the cooks will make Kishan's favorite meal tonight."

"Of course."

She placed her hand on my lower back as I rose. "Perhaps you'd like to walk in the garden? There is a maze at the center that is difficult for most people to navigate. I should think you can easily avoid your father's man there." Lowering her voice, she whispered, "The trick is to always turn to the left." With a twinkle in her eye, she departed along with her entourage, and when I was alone, I used my ability to become invisible. Taking her advice, I set out to explore the garden maze, something I'd longed to do.

The Rajaram garden was very different from the hanging gardens above the king's palace, but it was beautiful all the same, filled with flowers of every description and leafy trees that smelled of perfumed sap. Confident that I remained unseen, I took my time exploring, fingering delicate plants and flower buds until I came across the maze.

Curious, I entered and turned left a dozen times until I came upon the center. A fountain full of lotus flowers beckoned me closer. In the middle of the maze surrounded by hedges so tall I couldn't see over them, I felt safe, as if the plant life I loved so much could wrap around me and protect me from everything bad in the world.

Because I felt so secure, I let the power shielding me melt away and raised my face to the hot sun. When I became too warm, I shook the veil loose from my face and hair, let it fall about my arms, and ran my fingertips through the fountain, splashing the water on my neck and face. The humming of bees and the song of birds settled me, and I was able to forget where I was and, what was more important, who I was. In the garden, I was just a girl who loved flowers.

Among the pink and white lotus blossoms, I noticed something different, something I'd seen before. It was the same lavender water flower I'd found in the king's fountain. "Impossible," I whispered and reached down to pluck it from the water so I could examine it closer. "Perhaps you are more common than I thought."

A rich voice behind me said, "I would argue that it is exceptional."

Startled, I dropped the flower and turned. Standing at the opening to the center of the maze was the man I hadn't been able to forget, though it had been weeks since I'd seen him. I blinked, momentarily dazzled by his wide smile until he took a step toward me. Then I remembered myself and hastily pulled my veil over my hair and face then lowered my head.

He hesitated at seeing my reaction. "I apologize. I didn't mean to disturb you."

My tongue felt tied. I wanted to speak but couldn't seem to figure out what to say. Instead of demanding an answer or growing impatient with me, he approached the fountain and picked up the flower I'd dropped on the stone. Gently, he placed it back among the other blossoms. "It's beautiful, isn't it?" he asked, though he didn't seem to care if I answered. "I saw it in the garden of Bhreenam and asked for a cutting before I left. I thought my mother would like it."

"It's lovely," I whispered.

Tiny little fish darted to the surface, reminding me of the koi where I'd stood next to him earlier, but this time he knew I was there. As if reading my mind, he said, "There is a story told by my mother's people about these fish. Far away, there is a river full of them. Though it doesn't happen frequently, some koi fish will swim all the way to the head of the river. There they find a large waterfall, and the bravest, most unwavering fish that exhaust themselves by leaping to the top are given a gift by the gods."

"What would the gods give a fish?" I asked, quietly curious.

He tilted his head, and though I could see a gleam in his eye, acknowledging he'd heard, he didn't turn toward me but reached out and ran his hand through the fountain and then cupped the back of his neck, wetting his skin with the cool water.

"They are transformed into great dragons. The waterfall at the head of the Yellow River has thus been named The Dragon's Gate. So you see, any creature, even one as unassuming as a fish, can become something mighty. When they courageously endure their trials, they meet their destiny."

What he'd said was remarkable. Not only because I was wrapped up in his ability to tell a story but because he seemed to know exactly what I needed to hear. I, too, struggled against great odds, and I thought if there was hope for a lowly fish, then perhaps the gods were aware of me as well. Maybe if I proved my worthiness, I could be granted the gift I sought.

"I apologize for my disheveled appearance," he said, pulling me from my thoughts. "Kadam worked me over more than usual. I fear he punishes me for being gone these last few weeks. He thinks I've grown fat and lazy without his daily rounds."

As he loosened his shirt and splashed water on his neck, I swallowed and wet my lips but was otherwise frozen in place. Kishan was anything but fat and lazy. In fact, he was the most beautiful specimen of a man I'd ever seen. His arms and chest were thick with muscle, and his shirt clung to his body in such a way that made me feel like I'd been standing too long in the sun.

Speaking of the sun, his golden eyes, especially when they glanced in my direction, were warm enough to melt me into a puddle where I stood. In fact, I was surprised I hadn't pooled into the fountain already. I was imagining what it would be like to be the water he was splashing against his skin when something caught my eye.

It was the medallion. It hung about his neck, and I was absolutely sure it was the one my father was seeking. Cold fear seeped into my body, chilling my feverish skin. Wrapping my arms around my waist, I hugged myself. What was I going to do? If my father knew this young man wore the item he wanted, he'd kill him. Or he'd make me do it. Either way, Kishan's beautiful golden eyes would be forever closed. His warmth traded in for the cold of the grave. I shivered.

"Are you cold?" he asked. "Will you allow me to escort you back to the palace?"

I gave him a brief nod. He led me toward the open section of the hedges and said, "My name is Kishan, by the way."

"I know," I answered quietly.

Turning back to look at me, he gave me a puzzled glance but smiled. "I am at a disadvantage then. Perhaps the lovely young lady would grace me with her name?"

I stopped walking, my mind racing with the futility of what I was attempting to do. How could I save him, save his family, when my father planned such evils against them? I lifted my eyes and saw the cord at his throat. How would he die? I wondered. Would I wake one day to hear of black marks on his chest? Would he simply disappear? Or maybe his death would be at my hand. Perhaps I would be the one to draw my little knife across his throat. Perhaps I would be the one to press the cup full of poison to his lips.

Suddenly, I could look at him no longer. My name was the name of his killer. I was a murderess in the making. He at least deserved to put a name with the face of the one responsible. "Yesubai," I whispered. "My name, it's Yesubai." Crushing my skirts in my fists, I darted past him and ran all the way back to the palace without ever glancing behind.

Though I tried to avoid Kishan, he seemed to always know where I was. He was one of the only men allowed inside the women's room. I found him reclining at his mother's feet, talking with her, on more than one occasion. Each time, he tried to engage me in conversation, but I'd make my excuses and leave. When we dined, I'd catch him watching me, and he often volunteered for guard duty when I walked about the grounds to appease Hajari.

Kishan seemed to sense my relief at having him near, and when we walked, I almost forgot that Hajari was even with us. Kishan had the ability to make me feel safe. It was similar to how I'd felt in the garden. It wasn't just that he was a big man, it was something else. I didn't realize until the third day that what I felt around him was hope. No one could be around Kishan and not be affected by his steadiness, by the way he was grounded.

Like the trees, his roots went deep, and I daydreamed that if he wrapped me in his arms, he could safely tuck me away within his branches and hide me from the world. He was shaken by nothing. He feared nothing. Watching him spar with his soldiers, I could see that they respected and trusted him utterly. What was more, I was getting dangerously close to feeling the same way about him.

All too quickly, Deschen announced that the caravan was ready to take me to meet Dhiren. As I was loaded into the carriage, I lifted the curtains, seeking Kishan's face, but he didn't come to see me off.

I told myself it was for the best and settled in for the long trip to the far side of the empire.

When I met Dhiren, I was struck by how handsome he was. He looked more like his mother than his father. His eyes were startlingly blue, but as kind as he was, I missed the warmth of Kishan's golden gaze. We spoke at length. He was polite, well-mannered, everything a woman should want in a man, but there was something missing. There was a distance between us that felt too wide to breach. Though I watched him carefully during the time we were together, I never saw a cord about his neck indicating he wore a piece of the amulet my father sought.

It was obvious that the difficulties he'd encountered with my father's army had distracted him, but he never blamed me for the fact, and he didn't even discuss the diplomatic aspects of our union. He merely said he looked forward to our marriage and had a great hope that we would be happy together.

Documents were signed, and he was courteous and attentive in making sure I had every comfort he could afford for my journey back, but when he pressed his lips against my hand in farewell, all I could feel was regret. He was a good man, a wonderful one even. A man as different from my father as the night was from the day. That made my complicity in my father's plans all the more difficult to bear.

I hadn't been back to the palace for even a day when my father made another appearance, but this time it was an official one.

betrayal

A courier brought word to the palace that Dhiren approved the match several days before I arrived, and in anticipation of this announcement, my father had been notified. On the morning after my return, I was summoned to the hall of the emperor. Kishan nearly knocked me over on his way out.

He was angry—a not altogether uncommon emotion to experience when in my father's presence—but as he caught me, his eyes only lit on me briefly before glancing away. It was like he could no longer stomach looking at me, and the idea cut me with the pain of a thousand needles. I was so overcome by the feeling that I nearly forgot I was in the presence of my father.

Lokesh approached me while Kishan quickly left the room and disappeared. "Yesubai. How pleasing it is to see you in good health, my dear," he said as if he were happy to see me. But behind his public mask, his eyes glittered maniacally, and I could see whispered promises of agonizing things to come.

"Father," I said as I lowered my head. "I trust your travel has been without incident?"

"Indeed. Congratulations are in order. Your betrothal is cause for both our realms to celebrate."

"Yes," Rajaram answered. "In fact, we will celebrate tonight."

My father took my arm in a tight grip that was hidden by the folds of my dress. "Very good," he said. "Perhaps later tonight then we can discuss when you think your son might be prepared to finalize the union?"

"I assure you that his engagement to Yesubai will be foremost on my son's mind," Deschen said. "I'm sure that as soon as occasion permits, he will come speedily home to make her his bride."

Lokesh gave Deschen a saccharine smile that barely disguised a leer. "Until tonight then, I'll be reacquainting myself with my daughter."

Deschen's poised expression turned into a frown, and she rose from her throne. "If you wouldn't mind, I would like to spend some time with her this afternoon. I've grown quite fond of our chats."

"Of course." Lokesh bowed slightly and then turned and left the room with me in tow. He said nothing and even dismissed Hajari as we walked out of the palace and away from the rows of soldiers who guarded it. When he was satisfied that we were far enough away, he let me go and stood with his back toward me as he surveyed the land and the nearby garden. Putting his hands on his hips, he slowly circled, his eyes taking in everything around us until they landed on me. What I saw in his expression surprised me. He was...happy.

"You've done well," he said.

"I am glad to have pleased you, Father."

"Somehow you've accomplished even more than I hoped. It would seem your beauty is worth something after all."

I'd never seen my father in such a mood. He was almost dancing with delight.

"Not only have you finagled a marriage contract with the eldest prince, but you have his younger brother salivating after you as well. He practically begged me to consider him instead of Dhiren. I, of course, insisted that Dhiren was the better match. I wouldn't want there to be any doubt regarding your future station."

Kishan wanted me? The little knot of hope in my heart unfurled. For just a moment, I considered the way the emperor embraced his queen, and I wondered if there was even the tiniest possibility that Kishan might someday hold me in such a way.

My father interrupted my train of thought. "Deschen also looks upon you fondly. I could not have hoped for a better outcome. As such, I have changed my mind regarding our plan. You will poison the younger prince and his father tonight and wed the elder. If I can use him, I will allow him to live. He seems to be a competent enough military leader."

Kill Kishan? He wanted me to kill him? "No!" I cried and clapped my hands over my mouth as his shrewd eyes locked on to me.

"What did you say?" he asked in a low, threatening voice.

Scrambling to protect not only Kishan but myself, I said the only thing that I knew would distract him. "The younger prince wears at least one of the amulets. I've seen it. You must not kill him until we discover the location of the other."

My father paused and, emboldened, I stepped toward him and put my hand on his arm. "Kishan might be…manipulated. Perhaps I can learn of the other piece. Truthfully, I'm not sure I would have the same sway over Dhiren; he's kind, but he doesn't look at me with the same fire as Kishan."

"You are more cunning than I gave you credit for, Yesubai, but, then again, you are my daughter. Very well, use your wiles to discover the whereabouts of the second amulet and bring it to my attention immediately."

"What about the emperor?"

"What about him?"

"If I kill him, it would bring suspicion upon us. It will be much easier to handle the princes if they are lulled into a feeling of security."

My father stood rigidly, his body tense. He wasn't used to my talking back to him in such a manner, but he couldn't disregard my comments, either, and he still needed me to further his purposes. Blue sparks lit his fingertips. I saw them from the corner of my eye but knew better than to acknowledge his power openly. He squelched it and said, "For the time being, then, the Rajaram family will live. Work on the younger prince until Dhiren arrives and await further instructions."

Bowing my head, I said, "As you wish."

"Now return to the palace and spend the day by the queen. Speak to her of my…achievements." He then turned his back to me, an indication that I was dismissed, and I quickly headed back to the palace.

That night we dined together, one big happy family, though Kishan wouldn't look at me at all and my father watched me far too often. Hajari stood behind my father, his eyes shooting darts with messages that threatened me the moment he got me alone. He was one man I would feel no remorse whatsoever about killing.

My father was to leave the next day. When there was a knock on my door at sunrise, I assumed it was him, but, to my surprise, it was Deschen and she was alone. "Where is your guard?" I asked, fearing what my father would do should he come upon her.

Deschen shrugged. "Queen's privilege," she said with a smile.

She apologized for interrupting my sleep, though I hadn't slept for most of the night, and asked if I wouldn't mind acting as her companion. I followed her out to the open field where the soldiers trained. "What are we doing here?" I asked.

Shaking off her robe, Deschen revealed a fitted kimono-style gown buckled at the waist with soft slippers and leggings underneath like those a soldier would wear. "I needed some practice," she said with a wink. "Ah, there's Kadam now."

The middle-aged commander of Rajaram's army stepped onto the hard-packed circle of dirt used for sparring and handed his queen a gorgeous set of matching swords. I'd never seen weapons like them before, and I wondered if they had come from her homeland.

"My queen." The man bowed before her. "Are you ready to take position?"

"I was ready an hour ago. Were you curled up like a cat in his bed too long this morning? I fear you're becoming an old man, Anik."

The soldier smiled. "Not just yet, my lady."

"Then raise your sword," Deschen dared with a mischievous expression.

As they sparred, I curled up at the base of a tree to watch. The leader of the army was a skilled fighter, but it soon became clear that Deschen was more than capable of keeping up. I'd never seen a woman fight before, let alone move in such a lithe and supple way. The twin swords split the air as if they were an extension of her body, and she spun and twirled like a lethal dancer.

I could see why my father was fascinated by her. Soon the sparring pair was joined by Kishan, who good-naturedly teased his man-at-arms for being bested by a woman. When Deschen asked if her son could do any better, Kadam tossed him his sword. The prince tugged off his tunic and circled his mother. He hadn't seen me, and I drew myself farther into the shadows. Though Deschen knew I was there, I felt like I'd been caught spying.

The queen questioned her son as their swords met, and I soon wondered if she had brought me along for an entirely different purpose. Kishan, unaware that I was nearby, answered his mother's questions candidly.

She asked, "How are you after yesterday?"

"As well as can be expected."

"You know that we tried."

"What I know is that once again Ren wins."

"It's not a competition, Kishan."

"Of course it isn't. How could it be when there was never any hope of success? I will lose every time."

"Not every time. Perhaps it is only the father who yearns for the title."

"What woman would trade love for a throne?"

Deschen lowered her sword. "I would have," she said soberly. "Give her a little credit."

Kishan moved his sword to his other hand, twirled his wrist, and swung again. As their swords met, he was nose to nose with his mother. "Even if she wanted me, her father wouldn't allow it."

"We don't entirely know that's true." He gave his mother a doubtful look and she winced. "All right, so he's a stubborn man. Perhaps with time we can sway his thinking."

"Ren is due back within the week and he'll be expecting a bride to greet him."

"Perhaps there is something that can be done about that." Kishan raised his eyebrows at his mother's secretive smile and thrust her sword away from his throat. Deschen continued, "Whatever she decides, I want it to be her choice. I don't want to push her in any way." More quietly, she added, "The poor girl has been pushed far too often in her life."

With a skilled countermove, Deschen twisted her wrist, and Kishan's weapon was torn from his grip. She raised her sword to his chest and laughed. "Never underestimate women, my son."

Laughing, Kishan said, "I would never underestimate you, Mother," kissed her cheek, and went to retrieve his sword. "Best two out of three?" he offered, and mother and son began again.

Kishan's skin gleamed in the early morning light, and the care he took with his mother was heartening. Here was a man who would treat his wife with the respect and kindness he showed his mother. Here was a man not threatened at all by a woman of power. Here was a man I could come to care for.

Deschen was right that I cared not a whit to have the title of queen. I wondered what her plans were, and I marveled at how skillfully she'd played my father. She'd purposely led me there that morning. She wanted me to hear their conversation. I was considering why and what exactly she expected me to do about it when I heard a voice behind me.

"Beautiful." The sentiment of appreciation sounded filthy coming from my father's lips. I rose from my comfortable seat under the tree immediately, my cheeks flushed at the idea that my vigilance was faltering. That I'd been caught watching mother and son with same sort of thirsty desire that my father had, disgusted me.

"She is truly unique," he said.

"Yes. She is."

Kishan noticed us then and dropped his sword, earning a stinging cut on his arm when his blade didn't counter his mother's. "Yesubai?" He took a step forward and then stopped.

The queen turned, swiping her neck with a cloth. "Ah. Seeing off your father then?" she asked me with a wink. She addressed my father, "Thank you for allowing her to stay with us these next few months. It's a pity Ren won't be ready earlier."

I tilted my head, wondering what excuses she would use to keep Dhiren from coming home. It was obvious she loved Kishan, but I'd never gotten the impression that she favored one son over the other.

"Yes." Lokesh gave her a small smile. "A pity. Until such time as we shall meet again, my lady." He took her hand and kissed it for an uncomfortable length of time then turned to me. "Goodbye, Daughter. You'll be hearing from me."

Deschen asked Kishan to escort my father to his entourage of soldiers and then wrapped her arm around mine. "You held up remarkably well, considering," she said.

I wasn't sure if she was referring to the revelations I'd overheard or my father's presence. So I decided to say, "It was kind of you to ask for me to stay."

"Or have you return with him? I should think not. You're under our protection now, Yesubai." Together we watched as my father's horses pounded away from the palace and out the gate. Kishan turned toward us, gave me a long look, and then sighed and started back in our direction. As we waited for him, I overheard the queen's request to her man-at-arms, Kadam. "Increase security at the women's bathhouse. I was spied upon this morning. The villain has yet to be caught."

He bowed. "I will see to it personally, my lady."

Seeing my shocked expression, she quickly reassured me, "Do not fear, Yesubai. All of us will see to your safety."

Though I had every faith in the dedication of the queen's soldiers, I knew exactly who had been observing the queen. My face reddened at the knowledge of what my father had done, and I felt the guilt of it almost as thoroughly as if I had perpetrated the deed myself.

True to the queen's word, it was soon announced that Dhiren would be taking an extended tour of the empire. It had been suggested that he take some time to get all the empire's affairs in order before returning home and focusing attention on his bride. Dhiren reluctantly agreed and met with his father's advisors in towns and forts, taking the long way home from the war front.

Hajari had been left behind to supervise me, and because of this, Kishan took it upon himself to be my personal escort. As the days passed, I found I looked forward to seeing him. He taught me how to play Pachisi, and I became quite good at it, even beating him on more than one occasion. Sometimes his mother joined us, but more often it was just the two of us with Hajari sitting nearby, sullen and bored.

Deschen often summoned Kishan to the women's room, pretending she needed him only to ask him to take me down to the kitchens to fetch a sweetmeat for her or to escort me to the garden to cut some new flowers. Once she outright lied and said that I'd complained of being bored and would he mind teaching me how to ride. It was obvious that her intention was to purposely throw us together.

Considering the fact that I was to be married to his brother, the situation was awkward. Still, I relished being with Kishan. In the hours we'd spent together, I'd come to rely upon him. I loved seeing the glint in his golden eyes when he laughed, and the warmth of his smile filled my heart in an unexpected way. I'd never thought I'd be able to depend upon a man. The experiences I'd had with them had been less than pleasant, but Kishan was different.

Reliance soon became trust. Trust led to admiration. And then, before I was even aware it happened, admiration transformed into a longing that was at once terrific and terrible, and I realized I was in love. Despite this, Kishan remained as proper and as distant as a cousin.

As the long weeks passed and rumors of Dhiren's return began to circle, I wondered if I had somehow misunderstood Deschen and my father. That Kishan's feelings regarding me had changed with time. That he now accepted me more as a sister and no longer desired me as a man did a woman.

All the while, nearly daily, letters came from Dhiren. He spoke eloquently of the life he imagined for us together, and though my answering correspondence was brief and even somewhat curt, his responses to me grew warmer over time—more emotional and intimate. After sneaking out the secret passageway into the garden to avoid Hajari, I found a bench and was sitting there, the latest pages from Dhiren crumpled in my fist, and wondering what I was doing to this poor family when Kishan found me.

"Yesubai? What's wrong?" he asked.

He sat down next to me and pried the pages from my fingers. Smoothing them out on his thigh, he read:

My Dearest Bai,

The months we've been apart have weighed on me. How I wish I was at your side this very moment. Despite my mother's request, my intention is to return home after my visit to this town, passing over the last few stops. I may even arrive before you receive this letter. I must admit that every time I close my eyes I see you. I am the most fortunate of men to be betrothed to a woman as beautiful as you are. The way the light shone on your face...

Kishan stopped reading, the pages hanging limply from his fingertips. "Kishan?" I asked. "Kishan, say something."

He didn't. Giving me only a brief glance, he rose and quickly stalked away toward the garden maze. "Where are you going?" I called out as he disappeared behind the hedges.

I finally found him at the center of the maze. He leaned over the fountain, hands splayed against the rim, his back toward me, and he didn't turn to acknowledge me before speaking.

"Bai?" he asked quietly. "He calls you Bai?"

"Yes. No. I never asked him to."

"But you don't mind it."

I wasn't sure how to answer him. Isha called me Bai and I'd always liked the name. It felt like a secret between the two of us. It was a name meant for someone who loved me.

Finally, I replied, "I would prefer it if he didn't use that name, actually." Approaching Kishan from behind, I continued in a soft voice. "I know that you call your brother Ren, but I've only ever referred to him as Dhiren. Honestly, I don't know if I would ever feel comfortable calling him otherwise."

I was trying to convey to him in a small way that it wasn't his brother who I loved. Kishan still wouldn't look at me so I babbled further. "My father always said that nicknames are only used by lower castes of people." I winced at my own words. They sounded cruel, and it wasn't what I intended to tell him. I'd just insulted not only him but his entire family.

"He'll be home any time now," Kishan said.

"Yes." I answered.

"And then you'll marry him."

"Isn't that what's been arranged?"

"Is…"

"Is…what?"

"Is it what you want?" He turned toward me then and stretched out his fingertips, running them down the length of the veil covering my hair. The thin fabric, already loosened, dropped away from my face. "Yesubai?"

The way he said my name was almost a caress. My limbs trembled, and though we weren't standing any closer than we had in the past, I sensed the distance between us closing. The air wrapped itself around the two of us and warmed my skin.

"I…" My lips trembled and I lowered my head, unable to remain wholly myself while trapped in his gaze. "I do not love him," I finally murmured.

Kishan sucked in a breath and gently ran his fingertips along my jaw to my chin, lifting my head so I could drown in his golden eyes once more. "Do you love someone else then?"

Mutely, I nodded.

"Tell me," he said as I watched his lips form the words. My pounding heart made me feel overly tense, as if the only thing I could focus on was the tingling of my limbs. With a sluggish voice and muddled thoughts, I whispered. "I wish that you were my betrothed."

One heartbeat passed and then another, and the moment felt hot and frozen at the same time. Then he smiled, and it was sunshine and heat and unspoken promises wrapped in a single expression. Before I knew what was happening, he pressed his lips against my palm and kissed the tender skin. His lips moved over my wrist slowly before he took hold of my other hand.

The hazy fog that had enveloped my mind thickened, and I became a being of feeling and sensation. All I wanted was more. More of his lips. More of his warmth. More of him. He'd moved up to my neck when I was finally able to focus on his words. He had been saying he'd speak to my father.

I placed my hands on his chest and pushed him hard. Abruptly, I stepped away, and I felt the absence of his warmth as keenly as if my own father had frozen the blood in my veins. "No," I whispered.

"What do you mean, no?" he asked, as confused and as affected as I was.

"I mean, we'll have to be careful. My father is a…he's a hard man."

Kishan's expression turned stony. "I won't allow him to hurt you any longer, Yesubai."

"Please just… just give me some time to talk with him. Perhaps I can persuade him to reconsider." When he looked doubtful, I added, "I promise I'll try to find a way for us to be together."

"Ren will return soon. If we are to alter the terms of your betrothal, then something must be decided quickly."

"I will send word to him immediately." I took his hands in mine and pressed my lips to his fingers. "Please, Kishan, let's just keep this between us for the time being."

He agreed and escorted me back to the palace. I called Hajari to my side and sent him to my father with a letter saying that I must speak with him immediately. That night my father appeared in my room, and even though I had carefully prepared for his visit, my hands still shook when he appeared. "Dhiren approaches and is expected to arrive within a few days. Kishan has declared his feelings for me openly, and I believe that there is not much he wouldn't do to stop the wedding."

"I see," my father said. "Please go on."

"If you were to encourage him in his suit, it is very likely he will find a way to give you the items you seek. Perhaps then they would no longer be a threat to you and there would be no need to destroy them."

Darkly, my father laughed. "Do you think all this conspiring is because I see them as a threat? No, my ignorant daughter. They are as insignificant as your weak mother was. In the annals of time, the speck they make on history will be absolutely indiscernible. You think I care that he loves you? You think I cannot see how you pine after him. I am no fool, Yesubai. Make no mistake. I am completely in control of each and every one of your tiny little lives. What trifles I bestow upon you are because I wish it. That you exist at all is because I allow it."

He ran his hand over the stubble of his jaw. "Still, there is something to be said for allowing the game to be played out to its inevitable, heartrending conclusion. Very well." He gave me a final glance then turned toward the window. "Tell the younger prince I wish to meet with him tomorrow at dusk at the border between our lands in the space between the crested hills. I'll decide then if allowing him to live might provide me with sufficient entertainment."

I nodded, appalled by what I'd done, and as he departed, I was left wondering if there was anything I could have done differently. Again the silent comfort of sleep eluded me, and I used my darkest veil to hide behind the next day. Not only did it disguise my bedraggled state, but I felt like I needed it to cloak all the evils I'd been a part of. Not for the first time, I wondered if the world might have been better off had I not been born.

Kishan readily agreed to meet with my father and, under the pretense of a sunset ride, we set out to the borderlands. My father was waiting for us. He nodded to Kishan, who had approached wearing only a token sword and a breastplate. The fact that he was woefully unprepared to clash with my father did not go unnoticed by me. I bit my lip until it bled. Even if Kishan had been properly dressed for battle and had not approached as a petitioning bridegroom, he still wouldn't have been a match for my father.

After the proper genuflecting was done, Kishan announced boldly that he wanted my father to reconsider him. The glitter in my father's eyes told me that Kishan was behaving in just the manner he expected. "And what token will you offer me in exchange for the loss of the title?" my father asked. "Surely you don't expect me to indulge your proposal simply out of the goodness of my heart?"

Kishan made various offers of riches, fine horses, battle elephants, and any other trinkets he possessed, but it soon became clear that my father was growing bored.

"I have no need of such things," he stated flatly. "Kishan, I sense you are a man who can make hard decisions even if a sacrifice or two must occur. Am I right?"

Kishan folded his arms across his chest. "I am known for being decisive in battle."

"Very good. Then I will be as direct with you as I can. My daughter, Yesubai, has tried to set aside her feelings for you so that she might take her place as the queen and wife of your brother. Unfortunately, she appears to be unable to deny the budding love within her heart and would choose you. Frankly, it would be better for both our families and kingdoms if the two of you had never met, but I am a soft man who understands the passions of the young."

I raised an eyebrow but said nothing.

Lokesh continued, "Because I am sympathetic to your plight, I will agree to modify the terms of the betrothal."

Kishan laughed and wrapped his arms around me, squeezing me in a tight hug.

"But…" my father said, the disapproval over Kishan's actions obvious on his face, "you must agree to my terms."

Kishan stepped away from me, and the young man in love appeared to have been replaced by the prince worthy of being his father's son. "There is nothing I can promise you on behalf of my father. I can only give you that which I own. If there is something more you desire, you'll have to take it up with my parents."

Lokesh put his arm around Kishan's shoulders. "Son. May I call you that?" He didn't wait for Kishan's answer. "Let's not involve Rajaram and Deschen just yet. This negotiation is in such a delicate flux, we should proceed carefully. Hmm?"

Kishan nodded tentatively. "What are your terms then?"

"Oh, not much. A trifle, really. You see, I'm what you might call a collector."

"A collector of what?"

Lokesh laughed. "Many things, but in your case, there is something in your possession that might spark my interest enough to make me consider giving up a title for Yesubai a good trade."

"And that is?"

"There is an amulet in your family's possession. Two of them, in fact."

"The Damon Amulet? What would you want with them? They aren't of any monetary value. They're merely trinkets handed down in my family."

"Yes. I'm aware that they wouldn't fetch much of a price, but you see, they're very old." Lokesh smiled like a jackal. "And I have a special affinity for…old relics."

"I see."

Kishan lowered his head, his jaw working as he considered my father's proposal. Finally, he said, "I will give you my piece, but Dhiren has the other one in his possession. I doubt he would consider giving it up so that I might be able to steal his bride away from him."

"Yes. I can see how that might be a problem. Still, it's both pieces or there is no bargain. If we cannot come to an arrangement, then Yesubai will be married to your brother. However unhappy she might be."

Kishan said nothing but I could see the desperation in his eyes. As much as he wanted me, he knew there was no way Dhiren would voluntarily give up his amulet. Not if it meant losing me.

Behind Kishan I could sense my father gathering his power around him. If he couldn't manipulate the prince, he would kill him. "Kishan," I offered, "maybe there's another way."

"How?" he whispered. "Ren won't help us."

"What if we took him by surprise?"

"What do you mean?"

"Yes, Daughter. What are you saying?" I didn't miss the implied threat in my father's voice.

"What if we arranged a robbery?"

"Ren doesn't keep the amulet on him. Even I don't know where it is."

"So my father could send soldiers in disguise to meet Dhiren on his journey home. They would have specific instructions to discover the location of his amulet, and then they could detain him while you go and retrieve it. He'll never even know we were involved."

epilogue: fade

Things didn't exactly go as planned. Hajari and a few of my father's men stole me away from the palace the next night and took me back to Bhreenam, where Kishan met me with open arms. "What's happening?" I asked.

"Ren proved difficult. He wouldn't cooperate so he's being brought here. We're to greet him in the main hall when he arrives. It's not what we intended to happen, but Ren left us without any other option. Your father says we'll have to confront him openly and that he believes Ren will be more amenable if he sees the three of us as a united front. My brother is technically your father's prisoner, but he assures me he only means to threaten Ren until he gives us what he wants, then he'll sign a new betrothal agreement."

"But—"

"Ah, there you are, my dear. If you will excuse us, Kishan, I will escort my daughter to her chamber to rest and change before your brother arrives."

"Of course," Kishan said and squeezed my hand as my father pulled me away. When we arrived in my chamber, I let out a small cry when I saw Isha waiting for me. She was much thinner, and her face looked tired, but she was alive, and at that moment, it was blessing enough.

Pointing to the bed, my father said, "You'll be dressing the part. I expect you to look your best, and as such, you will not adorn yourself in your typical veil. I want you to be a distraction for both brothers. If you're very lucky, I'll let one of them live. But should my plans fail"—he stepped forward and cupped my face, forcing me to look into his eyes—"everyone you love will suffer. Do you understand, Yesubai?"

"I do."

"Good. I will send Hajari to fetch you. Make your preparations."

When the door closed, Isha rushed forward. "Oh, my darling girl!"

"Isha, I'm so frightened! He's going to kill them!"

"Don't you think about that. Just focus on one thing at a time. Let's get you dressed."

Two hours later, I swept through the long hall with bells tinkling at my waist and ankles. My hair was wound with gold and jewels. I'd never worn it uncovered before, and I felt naked without my veil, but I kept my shoulders back and my head held high. Kishan stepped out from behind a pillar.

"Yesubai," he gasped. "You look…you're beautiful!"

"Thank you. My father selected my clothing."

"Perhaps he means to allow us to marry immediately."

I gave him a small smile. "Perhaps."

"I promise you, Yesubai, we will find a way to be together. There is nothing I wouldn't do for you."

He touched his forehead to mine, and I boldly cupped his cheek with my palm. "I know," I whispered softly.

Even if my father did allow Kishan to live, I knew it was only a matter of time until he destroyed him and annihilated the small, fragile flicker of love that had grown between us. As I took Kishan's arm and he led me into the throne room, I knew it would be only a matter of time until he learned of what I had done, and he'd hate me for it. In trying to save the members of the Rajaram family, I'd only ended up chaining them to me so they'd suffer my same fate.

There was no way out. As I strode toward the dais where my father sat, I felt as if I walked to the gallows. The glimmering sparkle of hope had blinded me to reality, and now I sat next to my father, being swallowed up in it. When Dhiren was brought in, the certainty of my desperate situation practically crushed me.

He'd been sorely beaten but that didn't surprise me. If Kishan was shocked, it didn't register on his face. Ren was interrogated, mocked, and belittled by my father. That he was allowing his true nature to show through the carefully contrived diplomat he preferred to display meant that he indeed did not intend for the princes to live.

Shame filled me, and though it broke my heart to watch the tragedy unfold before my eyes, I was helpless to do anything to stop it. My father could not be beaten. I knew it and yet I'd deceived myself into thinking I'd find a way. I was a fool.

Through a mental fog, I heard my father say, "Perhaps you require a demonstration of my power. Yesubai, come!"

"No!" Dhiren and Kishan shouted together.

Unable to do more than shake my head, I saw my father gather his power to strike. He was going to kill. I had to do something, but every instinct I had told me to tread carefully. That my father would not forgive any form of treachery. I was frozen in place with terror. Then Dhiren said that my father's poison ran through my blood. I wondered if it was true.

Hadn't I conspired to steal from the Rajaram family? Hadn't I put my own needs above a stranger's? Hadn't I concealed weapons and poisons meant to slay the man I'd come to love? My father wasn't the viper. I was. I'd led these two noble princes to their deaths. Tears filled my eyes as I realized there was no escaping his evil. It flowed in my veins.

The knowledge of what I was, who I was, chafed. I didn't want to be Lokesh's daughter any longer. I wanted to be someone good. Someone brave and noble. Someone worthy of the love Kishan had offered. A pathetic whimper caught in my throat. If I did nothing, they would die but Isha and I might live. If I confronted my father, he would kill me along with them and then take out a slow, horrible vengeance on my maid.

My father continued, "Do you want to hear her scream? I promise you she does it quite well. I offer you a choice one last time. Relinquish your piece to me."

It was the lie that changed everything. All my life, I'd been deathly afraid of my father and his power. Every waking moment, I'd lived in mortal fear of him. When he announced to the princes that he'd invoked such terror in his daughter's life as to cause her to scream, I realized that it was that very thing that he wanted, and I'd never given it to him. I'd remained as stoic and unaffected on the outside as if my father were not a monster at all, but a man.

Though he had indeed traumatized me to the point of breaking me, he hadn't. He had never, not once in my sixteen years, caused me to scream. The idea gave me a sense of power like I'd never felt before.

Lokesh—I mentally vowed never to call him father again— had taken his knife to Dhiren and was weaving a spell. I saw light erupting around both of their frames. Before I could make a move, Kishan sprung. He crashed into my father, who used his power to thrust the prince away. As he tortured Kishan while a bound Dhiren attempted vainly to get to his feet, I noticed that Kishan had successfully wrenched the knife from Lokesh's grasp.

The screams of the two princes stirred something fierce inside me. Something needed to be done. Someone needed to act. I vowed then to be that someone. Against every instinct I'd built over my sixteen years, I gripped the armrests of the golden chair where I sat and stood up.

Feeling freed from the shackles of Lokesh's oppression, I lifted my arms, murmuring a plea to the gods that I might finally and truly be able to use my ability to heal and protect another. Like the koi fish, I used every ounce of energy I possessed to rise above the station I was born to and thrust the power I carried inside toward the two princes.

My secret wish was answered. I could actually feel the wounds my father had inflicted on them close. Lokesh bellowed in frustration as I shifted silently, becoming invisible, and grabbed the knife Kishan had dropped on the floor.

I didn't have experience with fighting like Deschen. I didn't have a plan. But I had a weapon. Lokesh bent over Dhiren, twirling his talisman, and I struck. With all the force I could muster, I sank the knife deep into my father's back. He shrieked in rage, and the sound gave me a moment's satisfaction, but the moment didn't last. I'd hoped that my attack would distract him long enough to allow the brothers to get away, but he wrenched the knife from his back and shrugged off the pain as if it had been the sting of a bee.

He headed toward Kishan, and becoming visible, I positioned myself front of him and thrust my hand against his chest, shouting, "You will not touch him!"

"Yesubai, no!" Kishan said weakly as he attempted to move me aside, but Lokesh was a tornado of fury. He used the power of the wind. It burst outward from his body in all directions, and as my father lifted me, tossing me aside so he could get to Kishan, the wind carried my body.

When I fell, my neck hit the dais and I heard a crack. I registered pain but only for an instant before a blessed numbness stifled it. Immediately the breath seized in my body. Everything stopped around me, and my surroundings took on a dream-like quality as an eerie silence descended.

I could see Kishan had gotten to his feet, but he seemed frozen, and I wondered if it was due to something Lokesh had done. Then I heard the tinkling of bells and a beautiful woman appeared before me. She took in the bloody scene of betrayal I had initiated and knelt down beside me. Her eyes were kind as she took my hand.

"Hello, Yesubai," she said. "I've always wanted to meet you."

She was dressed in a sparkling gown and her eyes were as green as a deep forest. She wore a golden circlet on her arm in the shape of a snake. After passing her hand slowly over my neck, she said, "You may speak if you wish."

"Who…who are you? What's happening?"

"I am the goddess Durga."

"A goddess?" Tears filled my eyes. My prayers to the gods had indeed been answered. "Then you're here to save us?"

Sadly, she shook her head. "No. That is not the reason I have come."

"I don't understand. Then why are you here?"

"As I said, I wanted to meet you."

"Why?"

"I wanted to get a sense of who you are." She glanced over at the men frozen in place and said quietly, "Specifically, I wanted to know if you loved him."

"Do I love who?"

"Kishan."

Perhaps I'd hit my head too hard and was in a sort of waking dream, but the vision of the beautiful goddess seemed all too real to me. And there was something about her that made me want to confess the truth of things. "Yes," I answered softly. "I love him. I'm sorry about what happened with Dhiren. He's a good man. He didn't deserve to be abused in this way. If I could go back and do things differently, I would."

The goddess studied me and then nodded. "I believe you."

"They don't deserve to have their fate tied to my own."

"I do not wish for you to worry over their fate, Yesubai."

"But Lokesh—"

She touched her hand to my cheek, leaned down, and whispered, "Your father will be defeated but it will not happen at this time."

"Will I live to see it?"

She paused, considered the question, and then said, almost as if it was against her better judgment, "I do not think as others do regarding knowing one's future, so I will answer your question." Taking my hand in hers, she enveloped mine. I only had a moment to wonder why I couldn't feel it before she said, "You will not live out this day. The fall has broken your neck."

"But I can heal myself."

She shook her head. "The gift of protection and healing you offered the brothers came with a great cost. In defending the two of them, the power within you was consumed. You became truly mortal."

Tears filled my eyes. She waited patiently beside me until I could speak again. "Have I proved myself to you then?"

"You have nothing to prove to me, Yesubai."

"Perhaps not, but Kishan said that a gift would be bestowed on even the lowliest of creatures whom the gods deem worthy."

The goddess hesitated then nodded slightly. "What gift do you seek?"

"Will you…take care of him?"

Soberly, with a hint of relief, she nodded. "I will. I will watch over both of the princes. This I promise you."

"Can you also save Isha?"

"Who is Isha?"

"She's my handmaid. Lokesh will take his revenge out upon her."

The goddess glanced up briefly, peering at something beyond the scope of my vision, and then nodded. "Yes. I will offer her a place of refuge."

"Then the sacrifice was worth it."

"Yes. Rest now, little one. You are very brave."

In a brilliant burst of light, the goddess disappeared, and once again, I found I could not breathe. Kishan gathered me in his arms, pressed his lips to my temple, and pled, "Dayita, my love. Don't leave me."

The gift of his heartfelt whispers and promises was something I wasn't entirely sure I deserved, but my heart filled with gratitude for it all the same.

The final regret that captured my mind as I was swept away from mortal life was not about Isha or Dhiren, confronting my father, or even leaving Kishan behind. The assurances from the goddess had given me some comfort regarding all of them.

No, the thing that I lamented the most as I lay dying was that when Kishan finally pressed his lips against mine, something I'd been yearning for since I stood next to him in the king's garden, I couldn't feel it. Death robbed me of experiencing the exquisite taste of his lips, but at least he was the last thing to encompass my vision as I departed the world.

BONUS CHAPTER:
Yuvakshi's Perspective
origin

he trembling girl drew her shawl tightly across her shoulders as if by doing so she'd be able to protect herself, but the bunched fabric made a flimsy sort of armor and in her heart she knew she'd never feel safe again even if she had been girded from head to toe in the strongest of steel. The seventeen year old stood in the warlord's bedchamber and pondered what had led her to this fate.

Her father's servant had unceremoniously left her at the doorstep of the king's military leader, a man even the most powerful of her father's friends had dared to whisper about only behind their hands. She'd known that her father, a merchant by trade, had recently made some influential new friends. How else had he become so suddenly successful? But she had no idea his connections went so high.

They'd always been well enough off, but Yuvakshi was the eldest of seven children and with so many mouths to feed, she had come to expect that her parents would make a match for her at a very young age. She'd held out hope though that the man she'd be given to would at least be closer to her own age if not one of the young men of the town who had shown interest in the past.

There'd been quite a number to choose from and Yuvakshi's favorite pastime as she worked with her mother or took inventory in the store was to dream of what her life might be like if she was matched to one of them. She had her favorites of course, most of those having a handsome form or a handsome wallet, or, if she was lucky, both. And her father was a clever man who kept his beautiful daughter in plain sight of all who graced his business, so she had plenty of opportunities to consider who might be a part of her future.

All who laid eyes on Yuvakshi agreed that she was a rare beauty who any young man would be proud to take as a wife. Even if she hadn't been comely, the sons from poorer families would have visited often, hoping to catch her eye and win not only her hand but a stake in the merchant's business. Any one of those hopeful boys, even the fat one with the ruddy complexion whose breath stunk of onions would have been a better option than this.

Yuvakshi had expected that when she left her home as an adult that she'd at least have an honorable union with a man who would take her as his wife. Not in her most fearful imaginings did she expect her father to use her in such a shameful manner. To give her away to one who intended to steal away the future she'd dreamed of. Nothing could be worse.

When her father announced his intentions, there was nothing Yuvakshi's mother could do to stop him. No amount of tears would change his mind. "A bargain is a bargain," he'd said, throwing his hand up in the air to halt the discussion before he abruptly left after issuing the cryptic instructions to prepare his daughter for her departure.

As the young girl was led outside with only her two finest dresses in a small bag, her mother wrung her hands and murmured quietly to her husband of dark things Yuvakshi didn't want to hear, but even she could see the fear in her father's eyes as her mother begged him to consider an alternative or to at least negotiate the possibility of an official marriage first.

Without even a goodbye, her father took hold of his tearful wife, clutching her to his bosom as he nodded abruptly to the servant who led the girl out of the market. Her steps were slow as she followed the man who wound his way through the busy shops and up to the main road. She was surprised as the business side of town gave way to homes that were more affluent and then they passed the residences of various diplomats and politicians. Still the man kept going.

Yuvakshi began to wonder at her circumstances. Perhaps her mother had been wrong. Perhaps her father had chosen well for her after all. Perhaps someone of substance had caught sight of her pretty face and selected her out of thousands to be the consort of a city leader. The girl bit her lip. Even if the man was older, it might not be so bad.

If he was an amenable sort, he might even consider marriage if she handled the relationship delicately. At the very least, she thought she wouldn't be hungry. It wasn't until she was led up to the nearly impenetrable gates of the king's military stronghold that she began to truly understand what was happening.

"Am I to be the consort of a soldier?" she asked the man walking beside her.

He scoffed. "Not a soldier. Your father wouldn't give you over to such as that."

She blinked and mulled it over before saying, "The king?"

The man laughed outright at that. "Do you think yourself beautiful enough to make him forget the wife he loved?"

Yuvakshi wasn't sure how to answer that question. To say what she truly thought would be considered boastful and yet if there was one thing she was confident about, it was her appearance. She didn't need to answer it turned out because at that moment the heavy gates swung open and the man escorting her gave them a quick salute before spinning around and heading back the way they'd come.

Suddenly surrounded by the king's guard, Yuvakshi had never felt so alone. She asked one of them to name the man she was meant for and not only did they not answer her, they didn't even glance in her direction. They were as stony and as unfeeling as statues. Uncontrolled fear spilled out in the form of trickling tears. Heavy doors were unlocked with rattling clanks that sounded to her like the weighted sound of a jail cell and even her stride felt slow and lumbering as if her ankles were manacled and chained to a heavy ball.

A stern faced woman met her at the top of a winding stairway. Being that close to the palace, and with the size of the home being larger than anything she'd ever seen, Yuvakshi thought the interior must have been opulent and grand but, instead, the passageways were confusing and dark. There was a distinct lack of windows and the ones she did see were made impassable with thick iron bars.

The ceilings were low and there were so many twists and turns that she felt like she was stuck in a garden maze where the plants were growing around her trying to overtake the path and smother those daring to traverse their borders. The woman sent to lead her had all the warmth of a witch who had been wrongly crossed.

She guided Yuvakshi to a room that was, if not opulent, then at least better than the corridors she'd traveled through. It quickly became obvious that this was not the space she'd be living in as her bag was promptly removed and a thin white gown was placed on the bed. The woman left with a warning that her master would return within the hour and if she was smart, she'd try to please him.

One last time Yuvakshi asked, "Who is he? Your master?"

The flash of pity the girl saw in the woman's eyes must have been a trick of the light since it wasn't there long enough to offer any comfort. At least she answered the question though. "His name is Lokesh," she said before leaving the room and locking the door behind her.

"Lokesh?" Yuvakshi whispered. Surely the woman was mistaken. The marketplace buzzed with rumors about the military leader who served the king. The atrocities he'd been said to have committed ranged from betrayal to the slaughtering of innocents. The kind ones said he'd gained power by making a pact with a demon but most of them said that he was the demon. How could this be? How could her father have given her over to such a man?

At least now the fear in her father's eyes made sense. If anyone had bargained with a demon it was her own kin. And she would be the one to suffer for it. Instinctively knowing that it would be wiser of her to play up her strengths with the aim being to gain any kindness the man possessed in his demon's heart, Yuvakshi carefully dressed in the gown given to her and finger combed through her dark tresses, pulling out the carefully woven braids until her hair hung in long waves down her back.

She smoothed imaginary wrinkles from the gown and stepped into the sunlight, turning her body so that the sun's rays reflected on her face and lit her eyes. The wait was long due to her nervousness but it was shorter than she would have wished. With a heavy clank, the door swung open and the object of her fear stood immobile staring at her.

Yuvakshi said not a word but straightened to her full height, angling her shoulders and widening her eyes before lowering her lashes demurely. "My lord," she said quietly and bowed her head briefly.

Boldly, Lokesh strode forward, grabbed her chin roughly and lifted her face so he could look at her. His eyes narrowed and his nostrils widened. "What is your name?" he demanded, his breath hot on her flaming cheeks.

"Yuvakshi," she said. "Daughter of—"

He squeezed her jaw, cutting off her words. "I don't care whose daughter you are." His hot gaze trailed down her form and back up to her face. "You're beautiful enough, I suppose."

"Thank—"

"Do not speak." Wisely, Yuvakshi held her tongue.

Lokesh turned away then and began removing his cloak. Then he sat and angrily gestured for her to help him with his boots. She did, but when she struggled to get them off, he thrust her aside. She fell against a table and knocked it over, bruising her hip in the fall. His hand had barely touched her and yet the push was so forceful, she could barely regain her footing.

At that moment, Yuvakshi knew two things for certain. First, the man she'd been given to was more formidable, more powerful than the rumors accounted for and second, he was a man with a violent temper who held no softness in his heart. Pleasing him would be the only way she'd survive, so she made survival her life's purpose.

She suffered no illusions about her place in his life. When she wasn't needed, she became as small and invisible as possible, but the moment he had use for her, she came to him and offered him all he wanted. It wasn't long before her former life seemed like a dream. Were there once people who loved her? Who wanted to make her happy? It seemed impossible.

Her whole world was now this man and the pain that hung around him in a black cloud. There was no predicting when the lightning would strike or how taxing and sore the punishment would be. If there was a pattern she would have discovered it. She was good at that. Good at sensing when someone was ready to buy or if they were just wandering the market looking to steal an apple or trying to finagle a better deal.

With this man there was no figuring him out. He was volatile. Angry at the world. And yet there was an incompleteness about him. He was...fragmented somehow. There was something he wanted and wanted desperately, but as carefully as she paid attention, he never gave away any clues.

When she discovered she was pregnant, she was hesitant to give him the news. On the one hand, he might feel as if her purpose no longer served him and he'd kill her. On the other hand, he might simply discard her instead. It was possible that her mother might take her in but it was unlikely. She was shamed and with child.

There were places such women could go, but the life of a tainted woman and her child would not be a happy one. Still, survival on the outside might be easier than life with Lokesh. She was worrying over her options, not finding an outcome that would be pleasant for her and her baby, when her master returned home. After helping him with his boots and handing him a cold drink from the water pitcher, she decided to simply tell him.

As she took the empty cup and turned, placing it on the table, she said, "I am with child."

She kept her back to him, the fear over his response turning her into a coward. When he didn't say anything, she hesitantly faced him. There was an expression of...not joy or happiness but... satisfaction on his face.

"Are you certain?" he finally asked.

"I am," Yuvakshi replied. "I believe it is the third month."

"With child." He mused as he studied her briefly and then left the bed chamber.

Lokesh didn't return all evening. The next day he found Yuvakshi and told her to prepare herself for marriage. He had arranged a wedding for them to take place the following week. Yuvakshi didn't know what to think but his reaction to her news was much better than she could have hoped for. She comforted herself by thinking that if she had to be wed to a demon at least her child would be born honorably.

That theme seemed to be reflected in Lokesh as well. He frequently made mention of his son being born legitimately. It seemed important to him for some reason and Yuvakshi hoped that if he bore no love for her then at least he might soften a bit toward his child. And he did soften…somewhat.

After the wedding, a small ceremony where her parents wished her well but studiously avoided looking into her eyes, Yuvakshi was given a more comfortable room, more maidservants, and, what was even better, Lokesh spent most of his time with her talking about the baby and her comfort, consulting with midwives, and gaining even more prestige and control in the kingdom than he had already. He said he wanted to build a legacy to pass down to his son.

Though Lokesh constantly spoke of a son, Yuvakshi ignored the niggling doubts she had over what would happen should a daughter be born. She hoped that he would coddle and spoil a daughter though that did seem unrealistically optimistic when she considered his character. Surely the gods noticed her quiet suffering and would favor her with a boy.

Sadly, it was not to be.

When her travails began, Yuvakshi relished in the hurt. It was nothing compared to the beatings her husband had given her before she'd announced her pregnancy. She knew that in giving him this precious gift that she'd be securing a place for herself and her child. Perhaps she could make this work after all. She'd try even harder to please him, to mold herself into what he wanted her to be.

The midwife said she'd never seen such an easy labor. As a servant wiped her brow and gave her a drink of water, Yuvakshi thought the gods had indeed blessed her. She heard the cry and saw the midwife wrap the bundle in a blanket. All Yuvakshi could feel was relief and satisfaction in giving her husband what he so desperately wanted.

Servants bustled about after the delivery and the new mother drifted off to sleep with a smile, a bittersweet and broken reflection of the beautiful and happy girl she'd once been. How sad it was that the little thing that made that smile possible, the tiny baby girl that rested in a cradle next to her, would be the last fleeting sense of happiness in Yuvakshi's short life.

The lovely girl, only eighteen years old, with long, dark hair and shining eyes of violet, the wife of a monster, woke from a pleasant dream to find her husband hovering over her, his face purple with rage. As he wrapped his hands around her, crushing her throat and stealing the breath from her body, she remained alert only long enough to discern from the threatening words he spat in her face that she'd had a baby girl.

In the brief, transitory moment found between life and death, Yuvakshi grasped onto one thought. It wasn't about what was stolen from her, or of her disappointing parents, not of her murderous, abusive husband, and not of the pain in her lungs. In those priceless and all too short seconds, Yuvakshi thought of the only thing in her life that gave her true happiness—the love she felt for her tiny, precious daughter.

And she was content.

BONUS CHAPTER:
Ren's Perspective
intended

The entire course of my life changed the day my parents visited and my mother asked if I was ready to become betrothed. Marriage was something that had not been at the forefront of my mind, but I agreed to consider it since it would help bring peace to the land and it was obvious she was excited about the girl. I knew that my mother wouldn't choose just anyone to take her place on the throne. The woman who would be my bride would need to be special.

I wasn't disappointed. Though…that wasn't how I felt at first.

Standing in the cool shadows of one of our holdings, high above the small but prosperous city below, I watched for my intended's arrival. The caravan arrived earlier than I anticipated and when I saw the carriage pass through the gates and under the decorative arch I was surprised at how my hands shook. That a mere slip of a girl I hadn't even met yet could cause me to quake like a green soldier in his first battle filled me with a strange combination of delight and distress.

My heart beat quickened and a heady sense of excitement ran through my veins. I was pleased to find that I was eager to meet my bride. Learning everything about her would be a welcome distraction from the constant skirmishes that plagued my mind. What would she be like?

I wanted to know her likes and dislikes. I wanted to memorize the way her hands moved and the scent of her hair. Perhaps I'd have enough time with her to discover one of her favorite dishes. I yearned to hear her laugh and wondered what she'd think of a future emperor that liked writing poetry.

As she approached, my thoughts shifted. Mother had mentioned that the betrothal, should I agree to it, needed to happen sooner rather than later, alluding to the notion that the girl was safer with us than she was with her own family. I frowned. Had she been hurt? Abused? My hands tightened into fists at the idea that someone had caused her harm. If I found that to be the case I would destroy whoever was responsible. That I already felt protective of her was a good sign.

The soldiers at the head of the caravan circled around the carriage as it came to a stop in front of the elaborate home that had become my temporary headquarters. Placing my hands on the carved railing, I leaned over and called out to Kadam's soldiers asking if there had been any incidents on the journey. They replied that the trip had been as easy as slipping into a hot bath, something the eldest soldier and leader, a man nearly ready to retire from the military, said he looked forward to.

As I assured him that food, rest, and a comfortable place to wash the dust of the road from off their feet was waiting for them, there was a flutter of curtains and I saw the retreat of a delicate hand disappear into the dark space within the carriage. Cursing myself for not being at the door to meet her immediately, I spun and leapt down the flight of stairs as quickly as I could and darted to the carriage just as one of the soldiers offered his arm to assist her.

Running a nervous hand through my hair, I affixed what I hoped was a charming smile to my face and waited for her to turn towards me. She was easily two heads shorter than myself and she was so swathed in fabric that I had no idea as to her shape or form. Seeing that she wore veils of sapphire blue, my favorite color, I took that as a good sign and said, "Greetings, lovely Yesubai. I am honored to meet you."

I bowed my head until I sensed she'd turned towards me and then lifted my gaze to meet hers. They were the most astonishing eyes I'd ever seen—a startling shade of lavender so bright they reminded me of one of my mother's coveted pinkish purple roses. Though a veil covered her face, it was sheer enough that I could see the curve of her cheek, her generous mouth, and her pert chin.

Despite the fact that I knew it was overly assertive, I couldn't help myself, and took her hand in mine, pressing my lips to her slim fingers. "I'm so glad you've come," I said warmly as my eyes caught hers again over the knuckles of her hand.

"I, too, am glad to be here," she answered in a soft, but distantly polite manner.

Too politically practiced to allow the wince over my careless blunder coupled with her barely lukewarm greeting to show on my face, I squeezed her fingers lightly, dropped her hand, and clasped mine behind my back and shifted several steps away. I'd assumed too much too quickly and had obviously frightened her. Perhaps she wasn't looking forward to the possibility of marriage as much as I was.

It was also probable that the idea of being near a man was alarming to her. I was good enough at reading body language to know that she considered me a perfect stranger, and one she didn't trust yet, but I was determined that I'd do everything in my power to show her I was worthy of earning it. And somehow I'd make up for approaching her like an untrained, exuberant puppy.

"Would you prefer to rest? I can have food brought to you if you would rather dine alone," I offered as we walked.

She considered my words for a moment and then answered, "No. I think I'd rather take my meals with the household."

Nodding my head slightly to acknowledge her words, I considered not just what she said but how she'd said it. I didn't get the sense that she particularly wanted to eat with me but she felt it was her duty. The last thing I wanted was to force a woman to become my bride who considered marriage to me an obligation. I wanted love. Maybe this wasn't going to work.

"We'll take our meal in an hour then."

She nodded and I signaled the women I'd employed to see to her needs during her stay. They rushed forward and bustled her off to her suite of rooms to see to her comfort. Sighing heavily, disappointment weighing on me but refusing to allow it to snuff out the hope I'd felt earlier, I resolved to give it and her some time and met with Kadam's soldiers as I waited for her return.

Dinner was a quiet affair with me doing most of the talking and her answering with brief words and barely discernable nods. My frustration mounted. This wasn't what I wanted. The girl I imagined spending the rest of my life with would have more fire, more passion, more…boldness. I wanted someone who would stand up for themselves. Who wouldn't be cowed simply because I was a man or the heir to a throne.

That night after dinner I paced the rooftop, wondering what I should do. Should I send her back? Tell my mother she'd been mistaken in her choice? It was true that she was lovely and she was well spoken, but that wasn't enough. Was it wrong to want more?

The moon suddenly broke from the clouds and I spotted Yesubai on the balcony below. She wore a gossamer gown of white with bell sleeves. Her shining face was free of veils and her dark hair hung loose, the ends of it nearly touching the ground. Strands of the thick stuff blew in the breeze. Again I was struck by her loveliness. As I stood there watching her, I saw her lift her hand to her cheek and swipe it. She did this over and over and though I couldn't hear a sound, I knew she was crying.

Was the idea of marrying me that awful? Did she feel trapped? Maybe she thought we'd cast her aside if she didn't agree to the wedding. Perhaps she would prefer to do something different with her life. She needed to know we'd protect her regardless. I was surprised my mother hadn't already explained that.

I headed down the steps and out onto her balcony. "Yesubai?" She spun to look at me in alarm. I held up a hand. "I am sorry if I frightened you. I was on the rooftop and heard your crying." It wasn't true. She hadn't made a noise at all, but I couldn't think of anything else to say. "Will you tell me what's wrong?" I asked.

Her lavender eyes were luminous in the moonlight and she looked like a nervous forest sprite ready to leap over the balcony and fly away at any moment.

"N…nothing is wrong," she answered finally. I could tell she was distressed that I'd been witness to her tears.

I took a step closer. "I promise you. I have no wish to see you hurt or unhappy. If the idea of becoming my bride is upsetting to you, it is easily remedied."

The panicked look on her face confused me. "No!" she declared. "I cannot allow you to send me away."

"That's not what I mean." I rubbed my jaw as I studied her, wondering why I seemed to be saying all the wrong things. It wasn't like me. I tried again. "I only meant that if you have no wish to marry, I will not force you. Nothing has been finalized. You are free to choose."

"Free." She blew out a short breath with a half laugh then froze and lifted her eyes to mine before turning her back to me. "If only I was," she finished.

"You can be," I said as I closed the distance between us. "Marriage to me isn't the only way for you to be rid of those who hurt you."

She stiffened. "What do you mean?" she asked.

"I mean…" I sensed she didn't want me to touch her, so, not knowing what to do with my hands, I folded my arms awkwardly across my chest. "I mean our family will protect you regardless."

"And who will protect you?" Her words were so soft that I could barely make them out, but when I did, understanding filled me. She was terrified. And not of me.

"Yesubai, I won't let you come to harm."

She turned and looked at me then, fully. No hesitancy. No reservation. Nothing hidden. It was like a window to her soul had opened and I saw the person she was. The person she wanted to be. She had a core of strength but it was buried so deeply within her that I wondered if she even knew it was there. I didn't know if I'd ever be able to bridge the distance and peel back the layers she hid behind. Even if it was possible, it would take time and a lot of patience, but I sensed the result would be worth it.

Quietly, I asked, "What do you want, Yesubai?"

She answered with a hesitant murmur, her brow furrowed as if she didn't understand the question. "I want…" she paused, "I want to be with someone who loves me. I want to live with your family. I want to feel safe."

I smiled then and offered my open hand. She placed her much smaller one in mine and though her fingers trembled, she didn't protest when I placed my other hand on top, and squeezed lightly. "I promise you. I will give you all of those things, if… if that is what you want, Yesubai."

She looked at our hands and then up at me, searching my face for a moment before saying finally, "It is."

That was the turning point for me. I had seen the person she wanted to be. The person of strength and fire who lived behind the veils. It would just take a great deal of kindness and patience to bring her out. I decided I could wait for that. I could wait for her to learn to love me. We could postpone a betrothal and even if we did decide to go forward with it, an engagement could last for years. I was confident that over time we would get to know one another and that there was a chance for us to be happy.

When I suggested delaying the betrothal the following day, she objected, saying we needed to sign the paperwork before she returned. It took me several hours of plying her with carefully worded questions before she admitted that it was her father that insisted upon the union. She absolutely believed that if she left without an agreement from me, he would cause great suffering.

I knew that her father was a clever and wily military leader and that he had manipulated his way into a kingdom, but now I also knew that he was the one responsible for terrorizing his daughter. That knowledge burned inside me, especially knowing that there was no immediate recourse to deal with him as he deserved. I would have to move carefully where he was concerned.

The important thing was keeping Yesubai safe and out of his reach. Taking revenge rashly or moving against the one who hurt her could undermine everything we were working to accomplish. Lokesh would terminate the betrothal at the very least and then use the excuse that we'd insulted him and his family to rain war down upon our heads at the most. I needed to think like the diplomat I'd been trained to be and curb the fire within my warrior's heart until the time was right.

Despite the political advantages our union would bring, I didn't want Yesubai to think that I desired a match with her simply to make peace between our kingdoms or even to protect her, though both of those reasons were valid. I told her that I looked forward to being a husband and pledged that I'd try my best to make a good one. Above all else I wanted her to be happy. When I said as much, she seemed to take me at my word and relaxed a bit more.

We spent a few days together and I was delighted that she wanted to be at my side as I visited the troops and met with city leaders. She remained shrouded in veils and was as quiet and as still as a statue, but I could see her bright eyes watching me as I spoke and she appeared to be alert and interested in everything she saw and experienced.

Hope bloomed within me again and I thought perhaps all was not lost. On several occasions I caught her staring at me, at the exposed bare skin of my upper chest and throat in particular, and I wondered if that meant she might be as attracted to me as I was to her.

I found myself smiling more often. I'd even penned a poem not about my mysterious dream girl but about the real girl with the long, black hair and shining face, who stood in the moonlight on the balcony with silver tears running down her cheeks. Though I never heard her laugh or discovered her favorite food, she did grace me with a beautiful smile or two and I counted myself lucky.

Before she left, I felt confident that we would be a good match and when I asked her once again if she was sure, she replied, "Becoming a Rajaram is all I could wish for." At her urging, the papers were brought in and we made our betrothal official. I knew my mother would be pleased and I was as well. Seeing her leave was difficult. We'd barely had time to begin the long process of getting to know one another.

I knew I needed to move carefully and slowly with her, so I only attempted the most courteous, the barest, of gestures and touched my lips briefly to the back of her hand, longing for the day when she'd be comfortable enough to allow me to hold her in my arms, and bid her farewell.

As I watched the caravan leave, I wondered at my newly betrothed state. We would be apart for much longer than I wanted. If there was anything I'd learned about Yesubai in the short time we'd spent together, it was that she needed constant coaxing, much like a hesitant mare, and I worried that the tenuous steps forward we'd made would be for naught if we were separated too long. It would be far too easy to let the fragile relationship we'd begun backslide to the cold distance we'd experienced at first meeting.

That was when I decided I'd write to her. Every day if necessary. If I couldn't be with her in person, I'd bare my soul to her on the page. Then, perhaps, when we met again, we'd feel that the distance between our hearts wasn't so hard to bridge after all

sneak peek from

tiger's dream

prologue: embers

Her wild heart raced, pounding chaotically like the stream she'd paused at. Her thin limbs trembled and as moonlight cut across her form, I could see her pulse throb and her eyes flick back and forth, alert to danger. I watched her from the shadows of the trees, a black specter intent upon her demise. After sticking her nose in the air one last time, she nervously lowered her head for a drink.

I sprung from my hiding place and tore through grass and brush, eating up the distance like a shooting star. My claws scraped against a gnarled root thrusting up through the ground like the arm of a rising skeleton and she heard the noise.

Bounding swiftly, the deer jerked to the left. I leapt, but my teeth caught only the thick fur of her winter coat. She let out a frightened squeal of alarm. Charging after her, my blood raced and I felt more alive than I had in months.

I pounced again and this time wrapped my claws around her heaving torso in a deadly embrace. She struggled beneath me, bucking as best she could as I bit her neck. Sinking my teeth in, I clamped down on her windpipe. Crushing it would suffocate her and I believed it was a gentler, more humane way to hunt but, suddenly, I felt as if I was the one slowly asphyxiating.

The exhilaration I felt when I hunted leeched away and I was left once again with the emptiness that constantly threatened to consume me. It smothered and choked, killing me unhurriedly in the same manner as I was taking the life of this creature.

I opened my jaws and lifted my head. Sensing a change, the deer lunged into the creek knocking me off her back in the process. As she disappeared into the undergrowth, cold water washed over my thick fur and for a moment I wished I could just breathe it in and let go. Let go of my memories. Let go of my disappointment. Let go of my dreams.

If only I believed death would be so kind.

Gradually, I made my way out of the stream. My paws were as caked with mud as my thoughts. Disheartened, I shook the water out of my fur and was futilely trying to get the mud out from between my claws when I heard a woman's laugh.

I whipped my head up and saw Anamika crouching on the limb of a tree, the golden bow across her shoulder and a quiver of arrows strapped to her back.

"That was the most pathetic hunt I've ever seen," she mocked.

I growled softly but she ignored the warning and continued making comments.

"You chose the weakest creature in the forest and you still couldn't bring her down. What kind of tiger are you?"

She nimbly hopped down from the thick branch. Anamika wore her green dress and as she strode towards me I was momentarily distracted by her long legs, but then she opened her mouth again.

She put her hands on her hips and said, "If you're hungry, I can bring down your meal for you, seeing as you're too weak to do it yourself."

Grunting, I turned my back on her and loped off in the other direction but she quickly caught up to me, matching my speed even as I darted through the trees. When I realized there was no shaking her, I halted and switched forms.

As a man I spun to her and bellowed in annoyance, "Why do you insist upon shadowing me, Anamika? Isn't it enough that I'm stuck here with you day in and day out?"

She narrowed her gaze. "I am as much stuck," she rolled the word across her tongue since it was fairly new to her, "here with you as you are with me. The difference is that I do not waste my life away yearning for something I shall never have!"

"You know nothing about what I yearn for!"

She raised an eyebrow at this and I knew what she was thinking. In reality she knew everything I yearned for. Being the tiger of Durga meant that the two of us shared a bond, a mental connection that linked us every time we assumed the form of Durga and Damon. We tried to give each other space but we both knew much more about one another than we were willing to talk about.

I knew she missed her brother, terribly. She also hated taking on the role of Durga. Power didn't interest her which actually made her the perfect choice to rule as a goddess. She would never abuse the weapons or use the Damon Amulet for selfish purposes. That was something I admired about her, though I'd never admit it.

There were other things I'd noticed that I'd come to respect in the past six months. Anamika was fair and wise in resolving disputes, always thought of others before herself, and she wielded weapons better than most men I knew. She deserved a companion who supported her and helped make her burden easier. That was supposed to be my job, but instead I often wallowed in self-pity. I was about to apologize when she started pushing my buttons again.

"Believe it or not, I am not following you around to make your life unpleasant. I am simply assuring that you do not hurt yourself. Your thoughts are continuously distracted which means you put your well being at risk."

"Hurt myself? Hurt myself! I can't be hurt, Anamika!"

"Hurt is all you've been for the past six months, Damon," she said more quietly. "I have tried to be patient with you but you continue to display this, this…weakness."

Angrily, I approached her and jabbed my finger in the air next to her nose, effectively ignoring the barely noticeable yet appealing dusting of freckles across it and the long lashed green eyes a man could lose himself in. "Let's get a couple of things straight, Anna; first, how I feel is my business and second," I paused then as I heard her suck in a breath. Concerned that I was frightening her, I backed up a step and stopped shouting. "Second, when we're in public, I am Damon, but when we are alone, please call me Kishan."

I turned my back to her, raised my hand to the trunk of a nearby tree, and let the angry fire she always brought out in me dull back down to dead smoking embers. Concentrating on slowing my breathing, I didn't notice her approach until I felt her hand on my arm. Anamika's touch always shot warm tingles through my skin, a part of our cosmic connection.

"I am sorry…Kishan," she said. "It was not my intention to anger you or bring your volatile emotions to the surface."

This time her irritating comments didn't bother me. Instead I laughed dryly. "I'll try to remember to keep my 'volatile emotions' in check. In the meantime, if you quit pestering the tiger he wouldn't be so quick to show you his teeth."

She studied me silently for a moment then walked past me, heading back towards our home with a stiff back. The fading sound of her muttering disappeared as she moved through the trees but still I caught the phrase, "I am not frightened of his teeth."

I felt a passing guilt at letting her return home alone but I'd noted that she wore the Damon Amulet and knew there was nothing on this earth that could harm her. When she was gone, I stretched and wondered if I should return to the home we shared, shared being a relative term, or if I should stay the night in the forest. I'd just decided to find a nice piece of grass to sleep on when my body stilled, sensing the presence of another person. Who would be here? A hunter? Had Anamika returned?

Slowly, I circled, making little to no sound and when I'd fully revolved I jumped back, my heart slamming in shock.

A little man stood before me as if he'd appeared out of nowhere, which he probably had. Moonlight shone on his bald head and, as he shifted, his sandals crunched the grass. We hadn't seen the monk since that fateful day when I gave over my fiancée, the girl I loved more than life, to my brother. The day I watched my dreams, my hopes, and my future leap through a vortex of flame and disappear, extinguishing like a lamp run out of oil.

I'd been depleted ever since.

"Phet," I said simply. "What brings you to my version of hell?"

The man took hold of my shoulder and peered at me with lucid brown eyes.

"Kishan," he said gravely, "Kelsey needs you."

DISCUSSION QUESTIONS FOR
tiger's promise

1. Despite the danger, Isha stayed with Yesubai. Was the sacrifice worth it?

2. Lokesh takes out his anger on his daughter and constantly threatens her. Why does he keep her alive?

3. Why do you think Yesubai decided to wear a golden veil to the king's party even though she knew her father preferred lavender?

4. Yesubai inherited powers from her father yet her father cannot heal or become invisible. Why do you think her powers manifested differently?

5. How does Yesubai feel when the king announces she will be married? Why?

6. Flowers and gardens are a theme in this book. Yesubai compares herself to a flower that's been shut away from the

sun. Are there other comparisons you can make between Yesubai and a flower?

7. When Yesubai drives up to the king's home with her father, she passes three gates guarded by animals—monkeys, tigers, and elephants. All of these creatures are found in the Tiger's Curse series. Were there any other symbols or references you noticed that are recurring themes?

8. Lokesh met Kishan in the king's hanging garden. What do you think was Lokesh's true purpose? Was it more than what happened on the surface?

9. Is Deschen different than how Ren and Kishan described her previously? How so?

10. The story of the koi fish leaping up a waterfall held significant meaning for Yesubai. Do you think she was truly granted a gift from the gods?

11. Yesubai wonders if the Rajaram family and the world would have been better off if she had never been born. What would be different about the Tiger's Curse if she hadn't been?

12. A theme for this story is "the apple not falling far from the tree." Is Yesubai doomed to become a villain like her father? How is she different from him?

13. Ren says that Lokesh is a coiled cobra and his poison runs through them all. In what way is this true?

14. The main theme for the Tiger Series is that true love requires sacrifice. Did Yesubai truly love Kishan? Did Kishan truly love Yesubai? Did he love Kelsey? How has he changed after his experience with Yesubai?

15. How are Kelsey and Yesubai similar and how are they different?

16. Is the opening poem "Early Death" reflective of Yesubai's experience? How so? Was her death "kind"?

17. Why do you think Yesubai was unable to heal herself at the end of the book? Could there be more than one reason?

18. Durga kept Yesubai alive long enough to ask one question. What was it and why was it an important one?

19. Assuming Durga had the kamandal and could have saved Yesubai's life, why didn't she?

20. Is Yesubai a different person than you expected? Do you like her more or less than you did before? Why?

ACKNOWLEDGMENTS

There are a few people I wanted to show appreciation for in helping me get this novella organized and ready to share. First, I want to thank my agent, Alex Glass, for his tireless support and effort on my behalf. I think he was nearly as excited as I was to get to work on this project.

Thanks to Cliff Nielsen for his beautiful art once again. You are an inspiration and a delight to work with.

Heartfelt gratitude goes to my early reading group. My sisters, Linda, Shara, and Tonnie. My mom, Kathleen. My brother, Jared, and his wife, Suki, and my friend Linda. You guys are all awesome and inspiring and you're always willing to grab an oar and help move this ship along.

Deep appreciation goes to my copyeditor, Amy Knupp at Blue Otter Editing, and to the e-publishing team at Trident Media Group, Elizabeth Parks, Emily Ross, Lyuba DiFalco, and Nicole Robson. You guys all deserve a party.

Finally, a standing ovation for all my dedicated readers, tweeters, and bloggers who constantly beg me for anything tiger. This one's for you. =)

ABOUT THE AUTHOR

New York Times Bestselling Author Colleen Houck is a lifelong reader whose literary interests include action, adventure, science fiction, and romance. Her first four novels, *Tiger's Curse*, *Tiger's Quest*, *Tiger's Voyage*, and *Tiger's Destiny* were *New York Times*, *USA Today*, and *Publishers Weekly* bestsellers. Formerly a student at the University of Arizona, she worked as a nationally certified American Sign Language interpreter for seventeen years before switching careers to become an author. Colleen lives in Salem, Oregon, with her husband and a huge assortment of plush tigers.

www.colleenhouck.com
goodreads.com/colleenhouck
facebook.com/tigerscurse
twitter.com/colleenhouck

Made in the USA
San Bernardino, CA
08 August 2014